FAMILY PRIDE: LOVE & CHALLENGES

Family Pride Book One

Deborah A Bailey

Bright Street Books
Piscataway, NJ

Deborah A Bailey/Bright Street Books™
Piscataway, NJ 08855
www.BrightStreetBooks.com

Publisher's Note: This is a work of fiction. Names, characters, places, and incidents are a product of the author's imagination. Locales and public names are sometimes used for atmospheric purposes. Any resemblance to actual people, living or dead, or to businesses, companies, events, institutions, or locales is completely coincidental.

Book Layout ©2013 BookDesignTemplates.com
Cover design by Steph's Cover Design
http://www.stephscoverdesign.com/

Ordering Information:
Quantity sales. Special discounts are available on quantity purchases by corporations, associations, and others. For details, contact the "Special Sales Department" at the address above.

Family Pride: Love & Challenges/ Deborah A Bailey. -- 1st ed.

Acknowledgements
Thanks to Kat Duncan and Kelli A Wilkins for editing and feedback.
As always, thank you to my mom, Ruth Bailey for her support.

"You can't be wise and in love at the same time."

−BOB DYLAN

1 THE HUNTER

Freedom. He craved it with every fiber of his being. Just being outdoors, running through the brush and letting the air fill his lungs was exhilarating. Taking loping strides, Mac pushed himself until his heart hammered in his chest. Stretching out his limbs, he leapt over a row of shrubs and padded down the trail.

Whenever he shifted into lion form, it always took him a bit to get used to his larger, heavier, fur-covered body. With muscles built for short, powerful bursts of energy, he always had to pace himself when running. No way was he going to tire himself out before he finished what he was planning.

Down at the end of the path, a two-level house was built into the mountainside overlooking the town of

Bristol Hills. Modern and spacious, it seemed out of place up here. No other houses were nearby, and hikers, warned away by tales of roaming mountain lions, seldom ventured near.

Slowing as he got closer, he sniffed the cool air. In spite of it being midday, it was always more comfortable up here. Lion shifters tended to stick to warmer climates, or places with lots of open space. Here in California he had both, and he couldn't imagine living anyplace else.

Now he was on the stone path leading to the house. The gravel against his paws was uncomfortable, but he'd used it to cover the driveway so he'd be able to hear cars approaching the house. So no matter where he was in his home uninvited visitors couldn't sneak up on him.

Pausing, he picked up the sound of water flowing. Licking his oversized tongue across his pointed teeth, he could almost taste the droplets. What was that smell? Lavender. Yes, that was it. She was up in the master bathroom taking her shower. Luring her here had been so easy, and soon, he'd have what he wanted.

Throwing back his head, he let out a roar. Maybe he should've waited. It hadn't been loud enough for her to hear over the water. Her hearing wasn't as acute since she was human and not a shifter. But he was desperate for her to hear him. To let anticipation build as she realized he was on his way to her.

It excited him to know that in a few moments, she would be his, unable to escape him. When she'd received his note, and followed his instructions, she should've known what she was in for.

Once he got to the front door, he shook out his mane and did a cat stretch, literally. Enjoying the power pulsing through his body, he was almost reluctant to change back.

Drawing in a deep breath, he filled his lungs and willed himself to leave his animal body and return to human form. Years ago when he'd been a young boy, he'd done it in front of his mirror. Watching his head changing shape, his whiskers and mane retracting into his skin had been fascinating for a kid of ten to see. But the ache of his sinew pulling and pushing, as his body changed from animal to man, had distracted him from completely enjoying the transition.

For the most part it was painless, but uncomfortable as organs and bones rearranged themselves. Not to mention the itching as his pelt transformed into human skin.

Even though the shift only took a few minutes, right now it felt like hours. He was hungry to be upstairs with the woman in his life, aching to feel her body pressed against his.

Down in the town of Bristol Hills, when he walked among the humans he was Mac MacKinnon, owner of Mac's Coffee Bar, the most popular coffee shop in town. But what they didn't know was that he was also a lion shifter.

Still on all fours, he stretched again and came to his feet. Another advantage of living up here in the hills was that he could get naked outdoors and not worry about neighbors. Clothes were restricting, and he always felt better without them.

Mac opened the door and walked into the spacious combined living room and kitchen. To his right the sunlight poured in through the skylights and illuminated the stainless steel appliances. His discarded jeans and shirt were in a heap on the floor by the couch. He'd thrown them there in his haste to go outdoors and get a run in.

Hopefully, she hadn't noticed his abandoned clothing. Surprise was more exciting, which is why he'd given her instructions to go straight upstairs and wait for him. She wouldn't expect what was coming.

Mac tiptoed up stairs, not making a sound as he ascended. At the top was the bedroom. Beyond that, his prey. When he opened the door there was no one in sight, but the bathroom door was closed. Like a skilled hunter, he sniffed out the terrain. Her clothes were on the bed. But he didn't hear the shower running. She was finished. Good. She'd be out soon.

He recalled his instructions to her. Be at the house by 11:00. Take off your clothes. Wait. Every part of his body was tingling as he thought about what was to come. It wasn't often that he sent his invitation for a little private time with her. They were usually much too busy at the shop.

But when he sent them, it was always worth it. And he had every intention of letting her know how excited he was that she'd accepted his request.

The door opened and they came face-to-face. Zora stood before him, her towel wrapped around her, her curly hair framing her face with dark brown coils. Startled, she gripped the towel, "I didn't hear you come in."

He waited a moment, not saying anything. Instead, he watched a bead of water roll down her bare shoulder. Guess she hadn't done much drying off with that towel.

"Did you go hiking?" she asked. "Wait--where are your clothes?"

"I shifted and went out for a run," he said.

"Oh...so that means..." A smile spread across her face. "I guess we're not going back to the shop for a little while."

"You know what I like to do after a run..." He advanced and in one motion scooped her into his arms and dropped her on the bed.

"Mac!" she cried out as she bounced.

Straddling her, he pulled off the towel and threw it aside. "Any last words before we have some wild shifter sex?" he asked, towering over her.

Laughing, she inched up the bed, trying to sit up. "We have to get back to the store in an hour. We've got work to do!"

"I'm the boss and I say we have all afternoon. You know how I get after I shift." He leaned down to nuzzle her neck. "I'm insatiable."

"If you'd told me you were going to shift, I wouldn't have come." Still laughing, she sat on the pillows and drew her legs up.

"Yes, you would've." He gripped the headboard. Nose-to-nose with her, he indulged himself by looking into her light brown eyes, seeing her excitement and her desire.

Her smile never failed to lift his spirits, no matter how tired he was. And when he gazed at the rest of her beautiful body, all he wanted to do was caress all the spots he knew would bring her pleasure.

At 6' 3" he was almost a foot taller than she was, with longer, muscular arms, so there was no way she was going anywhere unless he allowed her to. She was completely his, and the animal inside him was driving him to claim her.

But first she had to let him know it was all right. As much as he wanted her, it reassured him to know she wanted him just as much. After all the years he'd kept to himself as a nomad lion shifter, afraid to let anyone get too close, finally he had someone who accepted him as he was.

"What are you waiting for?" she whispered, as she ran her hands along his shoulders.

Gathering her into his arms, he kissed the side of her face. "I've been waiting for you, Zora," he said. "Just for you."

"Mac, baby. I've been waiting for you too."

Hearing those words overwhelmed him with desire. For so many years he'd been on his own. Mac had never expected to find someone who excited and challenged him at the same time.

He settled himself next to her, then brushed the hair off her face. "I was afraid you wouldn't find my message," he said, as he wrapped one of her tight curls around his finger.

"It wasn't hard. You left it taped to the desk! I'm glad I found it before someone else saw it. Why didn't you text me?"

"Leaving the note was much more fun. What are you worried about? Everyone at the shop knows we're seeing each other." Mac eased his fingers out of her hair and slowly traced the outline of her cheek. "Besides, I'm the boss and you're my assistant manager. What I say, goes."

"You're in charge at the coffee bar, not here," Zora teased.

"Oh no?" Maintaining eye contact, he continued to explore her. "Are you sure about that?"

"What are you thinking?" she asked, her eyes filled with amusement. "Why are you looking at me like that?"

"Like what?" he asked, feigning innocence.

"Like you want to eat me for lunch."

Mac brought her hand to his lips and kissed her palm. "Maybe I do." Instead of releasing her, he drew her index finger into his mouth.

"How do I taste?"

"Sweet, as usual." All this playing was fine, but hunger was gnawing at him, making him ache to taste more of her.

"Mac, when you shift, does it hurt?" she asked.

"Huh?" Normally she didn't ask a lot of questions about shifting. Seemed like a strange time to bring it up. "It can be uncomfortable. I'm used to it."

"But where do shifters come from? How did they evolve?" Zora eased her hand out of his grasp and rested it on his chest.

This was getting in the way of the mood. "Why all these questions?"

"Mac, we've been seeing each other for three months now. There are things I want to know."

"Are you afraid of me?" he asked. Maybe that's what this was about. She wasn't comfortable being with him and didn't want to say it. It was the thing he'd feared since he'd revealed himself to her.

"Of course not." She ran her finger down the middle of his chest. "I wouldn't be here if I was."

He shivered as the tip of her fingernail made contact with his flesh. "That's what I want to hear." It was time to get her mind on more important things.

Easing her onto her back, he gave her a kiss on her deliciously full lips, losing himself in the sensation of her tongue teasing his.

There'd be enough time for talking later.

When Mac woke, the afternoon sun was so bright he wished he'd closed the blinds before they'd gone to bed. Turning his back to the row of windows, he stretched and settled himself as close to Zora as possible.

"I'm hungry," he said. Spooning with her after sex always made him hungry for some reason. Maybe because he couldn't help himself from nibbling on her shoulder.

She brushed him away. "I thought lions didn't like eating people."

As he'd expected, the mid-morning run had done wonders for him. After putting in so many hours at the shop, and finding a new location for his second one, he'd needed a break. But with Zora here, he certainly wasn't getting any rest. Since she'd come into his life, he'd given up control over his body and his heart.

He glided his teeth against her skin before giving her another bite. "Depends on the person."

"Mac!" She tried to scoot away, but his strong arm held her close. "Keep that up and next time I'm bringing a bottle of ketchup."

"That sounds like fun. But whipped cream might be better." He kissed her ear, and then began to nibble her lobe.

"Stop! Haven't you had enough?" she asked.

"If I fix us something to eat, we can come back to bed afterwards."

"Is that all you think about?"

"No, I think about the shop, and then I think about sex again," Mac replied.

"You didn't answer my question before about the shifters. How did they evolve?"

"That again?" He sighed. Why did she wait until they were in bed to talk about this stuff? "We evolved just like humans did. Shifters and humans lived together, then the people in power started to hunt us. They said we were evil and had to be destroyed. Different shifter groups claimed their territories and went underground."

"How long ago?" she asked, settling herself on his pillow. "Why isn't there anything written down about it?"

"I don't know. It was centuries ago. I'm not a historian, Zora. I just know what my grandmother told me." Stories had been passed down, but he hadn't paid much attention when they'd been shared. It was all so long ago, and truth be told, history always bored the hell out of him.

"But don't you wonder about it? I've heard stories about shifters in Bristol Hills since I was a kid, but I never met one," she said.

"As far as you know," Mac retorted. But she was right about the stories. In the surrounding towns, everyone knew about the legends and alleged sightings. It had given the area a bit of notoriety. From time to time, some supposed "shifter investigator" would show up with cameras and equipment. They'd cause a stir in the community, but with no real proof, nothing much would ever come of it.

Hiding in plain sight came easily to shifters. Self-preservation was something they were very good at.

"But, Mac--"

"Enough, babe. It's time for another snack." He nuzzled her again, while he attempted to straddle her.

Wiggling away from him, she almost got to the other side of the bed before he grabbed her.

He began to tickle her. Getting all the places he knew she'd be helpless to do anything but dissolve into fits of laughter.

When he'd met Zora, his social life had been non-existent, and he'd been resigned to never finding someone who could claim his heart.

But in just three months his life had completely changed.

"Mac, stop tickling me. Let's go eat." She gripped his shoulders. "You said you were going to put something on the grill."

"I'm not hungry for that anymore." No, he wanted something else entirely now.

"We've got to get up sooner or later," she protested, gasping as he squeezed her breast.

"Later," he whispered. Nature was very kind to shifters. He wasn't exactly insatiable, but he had a lot of stamina. And another thing that made Zora so perfect was that she did too.

Easing himself down, he was about to plant a kiss between her breasts when the doorbell chimed.

She jumped. "Are you expecting anyone?"

"No, damn it!" Breathing hard, he composed himself, trying to decide if he should answer it or not. Everything in him wanted to finish what he'd started, but he knew that wasn't practical. If he had a visitor, it had to be important. It's not like someone would come all the way up here for no reason.

"Maybe something happened at the shop," Zora offered.

"No, they would've called. I'll go see who it is." He rolled off the bed and went over to grab a pair of jeans. "I'll be right back."

He closed the door behind him and headed down the stairs. Who the hell was coming here unannounced? When he opened the door, he had a shock.

"Hey there, brother!" It was his baby brother, Chris. Shorter than Mac by about half a foot, he looked more boyish than his 30 years. His curly blonde hair was tousled, looking like he'd just rolled out of bed, which for him wasn't unlikely.

"Who belongs to that other car outside? Got company?" Grinning, he strolled in and dropped his backpack on the floor. "Hope I'm not interrupting anything."

"Why are you here? Something wrong at home?" It was like his brother to show up like this. Ordinarily, he'd be happy to see him after not visiting his family in over two years. But this was not the best time.

"Well, I do have a message." Chris shoved his hands into the pockets of his hoodie. "Mom and Dad need your help and want you to come home right away. So drop whatever it is you're doing and let's go."

2 UNEXPECTED GUEST

"Chris, what the hell is going on? If Mom and Dad needed me, they could've called. Is this a trick to get me to go back there?"

"There's a challenge coming. Mom and Dad want you home for it." Chris pointed to the flat screen TV. "Hey, that's cool. How big is it?"

"My life's here, Chris. I'm not looking to lead the pride. Mom and Dad know that."

"Dad's stepping down." He pulled out one of the counter stools and perched on the edge. "Is this real granite? That's a big fridge. How about some lunch? I'm hungry."

Typical Chris. "This isn't a restaurant."

His brother ignored him and continued to survey the room. "Hey, where'd you get the couch? Kind of beat up, though. Why don't you get some new furniture?"

"Stay out of my business. I'm still not going back with you," Mac said. He'd left home and made his own life. He was fine right where he was.

"So you're going to stay a nomad? All by yourself?" Chris asked.

Of course his brother didn't know about Zora, and neither did anyone else in his family. It had been enough to tell her he was a shifter. He wasn't ready to add family drama into the mix.

"I'm not alone, Chris. Besides, Grandma's just a half hour away in Hermosa." And just like Bristol Hills, it had a large shifter population.

Chris shook his head. "You sound like you blame Mom and Dad. You made the choice to leave."

Yeah, he had made the choice. But deep down he knew it had been best because if he'd stayed, one day he would've had to challenge his father's leadership. It was better this way.

"So, where's your guest?" Chris inclined his head towards the stairs. I'm guessing it's a female. Did Grandma introduce you to one of those nice, boring girls from the Mathison pride? They're in this area someplace, I think."

"She's not from a pride. She's human." Mac folded his arms across his chest, preparing himself for his brother's reaction.

"So she's human. So what? So's mom," Chris said.

"Yeah, but you know everyone wasn't happy about that," Mac remarked.

"Grandma was okay with it, and she's got the seniority in the pride. You care about those snooty shifters? Our family's just as old and we've got more land and money."

"It's not always about money and property, Chris. They're all about tradition," Mac said. "Besides, I got tired of all those lionesses who only wanted me for the MacKinnon name. None of that means anything to Zora."

"I think they wanted you for more than that, brother." Chris chuckled. "The status was extra."

"Right." It wasn't like he was unaware of his looks, or the status of being an alpha male lion shifter-- especially one with an old family name. But to think that he was being appraised by people who only wanted him for those things, pissed him off.

That was one of the things that had drawn him to Zora. She was completely outside of the shifter world and she loved him for him, not for his family name or his status. She had no problem standing up to him, and that was exciting. Even though his true nature was to lead, he didn't want his mate to be a follower;

he wanted a partner and a lover. Otherwise, what was the point?

"Sure she won't tell anybody you're a shifter?"

"We're honest with each other. I know I can trust her." He would never have revealed anything if he didn't think she could be trusted. There was no telling what the humans would do if they could prove that shifters existed. His people had been hunted once, and that time could come again if they weren't careful.

"I knew you'd hook up with someone eventually." Chris' smile was so wide it seemed to take up his entire face. "It's not healthy being alone all the time. You've got to work off that excess energy."

"I'm not with her just for sex."

"You act like being with her for sex is a bad thing," Chris said, as he slid off the stool. "So, where is she? Can I meet her?"

Now what? Was he ready to introduce Zora to his brother? "Look, if she comes down here, no smart ass shit--got it?"

"I promise," he said, holding up one hand and placing the other on his heart. "I'll behave. By the way, can I stay here? Why didn't you ever send pictures of this place? The house is great. Can't say much about your taste in furniture, though."

"No, you can't stay." Mac didn't wait for his brother's reply. Instead he ran up the stairs and paused at the bedroom door. He took a deep breath before he entered the room.

Zora was sitting up in bed, the sheet covering her breasts. "Who's down there?"

"My brother, Chris decided to drop in," he replied. "I can get rid of him."

"Weren't you going to cook something? I'll come down and you can fire up the grill." She threw the covers back and eased over to the edge of the bed.

Mac sped over and got to her as she stood up. "He can be a pain. I don't want you to feel like you have to meet him." He took her into his arms. "Maybe we should wait."

"Are you afraid of something?" she asked.

"No, of course not."

"Then I'll come down."

"No, you don't have to. Wait here. I'll get rid of him." Entertaining his brother was not what he'd planned for their time together.

"Mac, you sound like you're afraid of him meeting me."

If he kept pressing it, she'd think something was wrong with her. And that wasn't it at all. He just didn't want to mess things up now that they were going so good. "Come down when you're ready. But after we eat, he's out."

"So, since when do you need an assistant manager? It's just a coffee shop."

Mac took the steaks out of the fridge and set them down next to the bowl of ground beef. He'd bought a house in a town far from the pride so he wouldn't get regular visits. But he should've known there was no escape where family was concerned.

"Chris, it's not just a coffee shop. It's a profitable business, and I have a new location about to open. Okay?" Mac didn't know what was worse. Explaining his hiring decisions to his little brother, or having to put up with his stupid questions. "She's going to manage the place. That way I can spend more time at the new shop."

"Is she coming down soon? I have a lot of stories to tell her about you." Chris grinned, showing off his perfect smile.

As Mac remembered, that smile had gotten Chris out of a lot of punishments when they'd been growing up. His younger brother's combination of charm and boyishness had saved him more often than it should've.

"I told her to take her time."

"Now I know why you haven't introduced her to anyone," Chris replied, reaching across the counter to grab a handful of raw ground beef. "You think your shifter family will scare her away."

"Zora knows she has nothing to fear from me." Mac pushed the bowl out of his brother's reach.

"Maybe. But she hasn't seen you the way I have." Chris dropped the meat into his mouth.

"Look, Zora is a civilian. Don't embarrass me."

"Brother, I would never do anything to mess this up for you," Chris said. "But I knew you couldn't do the nomad thing forever. You haven't had a mate since high school."

"Ali wasn't a mate. She was a girlfriend." Mac picked up the containers of meat and took them over to the cooktop. "You know it's not the same thing."

"I'm glad you're letting Zora meet me. I didn't even know you were seeing Ali until after you broke up." Chris chuckled.

"Zora makes her own decisions, Chris. And you don't know anything about me and Ali. You were a kid." He turned on the burner and set a cast iron skillet on top of the fire.

One benefit of spending his college years with his grandmother was that he'd learned how to cook. That's what had led him to invest in a very expensive kitchen remodel when he'd bought the house. Cooking was a big stress reliever. Then again, so was sex.

"So here you are, an old man of thirty-five and finally you realize what you've been missing," Chris said. "I guess walking away from the pride and becoming a nomad wasn't much fun after all."

"You've been spending too much time listening to bullshit." Mac threw one of the steaks into the pan, where it popped and sizzled. "I have this house and a successful business, little brother. I had my own dreams to follow."

"You were supposed to come home after you earned that MBA, brother." Chris emphasized the last word. "Not run off on your own. Dad expected you to come back and work in the business."

"A vineyard? That's Dad's dream, not mine." Mac pulled a large fork out of the drawer next to the stove. "Why don't you join the business?"

"I'm not the business type. Anyway, you're the oldest son, Mac. I'm just the pesky little brother."

Mac heard Zora walking upstairs. Shit. He wasn't ready for this. He turned down the fire and placed the lid on top of the pan.

A moment later he saw Zora's feet as she descended the stairs. Where were her shoes? Glancing around the room he noticed one of her gold sandals mixed in with a small pile of footwear. His habit of leaving his shoes by the door was rubbing off on her.

Zora wore a long, sleeveless dress with bright red and gold flowers. He hadn't seen this dress before, and he liked how it made her look. Mac rushed around the counter and met her at the bottom stair.

"Zora, this is my brother, Chris. He's the baby of the family."

"Hi there, Chris."

She extended her hand, but before his brother could grasp it, Mac nodded to the sink. "Why don't you wash your hands first?"

"What? Why?" Chris wiped his hands on his jeans. "Since when do I need to wash my hands? It was just meat."

Mac sighed. Just great. He knew it wouldn't take long for his little brother to make him crazy.

"Nice to meet you, Zora." Chris shook her hand. "It should be obvious that I'm not just the younger brother, but the better looking one."

"How much younger are you?" she asked.

"Five years," Chris replied. "What about you? Got brothers and sisters?"

"Oh, I...um...I have a sister and a brother-in-law," she stammered. "Um, I'm really thirsty. Can I have some water or something?"

"Sure, I'll get you some." Mac led her to the kitchen counter. Why was Chris so damned nosey? Couldn't he tell Zora was uncomfortable?

"Something smells good," she said.

Mac poured a glass of water and set it in front of her. "Steak. My specialty."

Chris sat next to her. "Mac's a good cook, especially steak. You know, there's nothing like a red juicy steak with the blood dripping. Do you like rare meat?"

"Um...usually not that...juicy."

"Chris, do you think maybe you should go check the grill out back? I think I left it on. In fact, we can go together and check it." Mac rushed around the counter and dropped his large hand on his brother's shoulder.

"I'm sure you turned it off, brother." Chris slid off the stool. "But before I go, Zora, how do you feel about really hairy men? I think I can guess, but are you for or against?"

"What?"

"Chris!" Mac yanked him so hard he almost went flying. "Come with me now."

"I was just asking!" He grabbed his backpack and slung it across his shoulder. "If you saw his hairy ass and you didn't run screaming, it must be love."

"Damn it, Chris!" Mac roared, cuffing him on the side of the head for extra emphasis. "You're out of here now."

"Is everything all right?" Zora asked, a worried expression on her face.

"It's fine. I'll be right back. Say, bye, Chris."

"Bye, Zora!" Chris called, as Mac opened the door and pulled him outside.

Zora took a sip of water and composed herself. The look on poor Mac's face had been priceless. For a moment it looked like he was going to throw his brother out the door head first. Chris was a handful.

But even worse, she'd almost revealed a secret she'd been keeping from him. Chris' question about her family had been innocent enough, but it'd caught her off guard. Mac still didn't know how she'd happened to turn up at his shop that day. He thought she'd come because of the job ad, but she'd really come because she'd discovered who he was and wanted to meet him.

After seeing him visit his vet, who happened to be her sister, she'd wanted to know who he was. So, taking advantage of her chance to look through her sister's files, she'd discovered Mac's shifter identity.

But the price for that was not telling him how she'd found out--and not telling her sister that she was dating Mac.

If he found out the truth, how would he react? Would he be angry or feel betrayed? She had a feeling that pissing off a lion shifter wasn't the best idea. He trusted her, and it was better to keep it that way.

She heard a car rolling across the gravel, and Mac's voice calling something. Then the door opened and he came back inside.

"Sorry about that," he said. "My brother likes to joke." Mac still looked pained and unsure of her reaction.

"It's okay. I thought you were going to feed me."

He brightened. "Yeah, that's a good idea. Let me check the steak and we can throw a salad together."

Zora sat at the counter and watched Mac prepare the food. It was hard not to admire him, especially with his shirt off. His abs certainly didn't come from spending hours in the gym, and neither did his muscular arms. As he'd explained it to her, shifting into lion form burned tons of calories and kept his human body trim and toned.

Even though he spent a lot of time working at the coffee bar, the light tan on his skin came from his hours working on the landscaping around his house. He wasn't the type to be happy sitting at a desk. If he wasn't exerting himself in some way, as a human or lion, he wasn't happy.

He turned back to the counter and broke into a smile as he grabbed the bowl of ground beef. "I'll make up a few burgers in case there's not enough steak."

"You mean not enough steak for you," she teased.

Leaning across the counter, he puckered his lips. She responded by meeting him halfway and giving him a quick kiss.

Zora enjoyed the meal. It was delicious, as usual. She loved Mac's cooking, especially his desserts. At least she'd get to have some of the leftover cobbler she knew was in the fridge. He'd served it after dinner a couple of nights ago.

"Mac, have you thought about selling any of your desserts at the shop?" she asked.

"You think they're that good?" He picked up the bowls and put them in the sink.

"The cobbler we had the other night was really good."

He opened the dishwasher and began to load it. "Maybe when I get the other shop open I'll put it on the menu."

"I hope you think about it." Zora put her empty beer bottle into the recycle bin. "Now that you've fed me, I feel like taking a nap."

Mac chuckled. "I think I'll join you. But first I'm going to call the shop and make sure everything's okay."

"You have to trust them to do their jobs. They've all been working for you since you opened," Zora said.

"I'm not used to taking time away." He closed the dishwasher and stood there looking down at the counter. "Feels strange."

Zora went over and put her arms around him, pressing herself against his bare back. "Mac, I love to work, too and I love the shop, but you do need time for yourself. That's why I was surprised to get your note. You usually don't take time off in the middle of the day."

After three months together, she had a feel for when he needed time alone and when he wanted company. Part of him was always going to be the nomad, even he acknowledged that. But she was concerned he was pushing himself too hard.

If she could only get him to accept the systems she was putting in place, he wouldn't have to put in so many hours.

"Want to take a walk?" he asked.

"Yes, let's."

Outside was peaceful, with only the sound of birds chirping. No car horns or city noises. A perfect place to be secluded, especially for a person who wanted his privacy.

"I love it up here," she said. His property had a trail for hiking up into the hills, and a shrubbery-lined path that circled the house. From the back patio, they could look down on the town below. At night, it was like looking at a grid of twinkling lights.

"Well, I asked you to move in," Mac replied, stooping down to pick up a stick. "Then you can be here everyday."

She'd been surprised when he'd brought it up, especially since it hadn't been long after he'd revealed he was a shifter. "You're used to your privacy."

"I know, but I told you, lions don't date for long periods. We see a mate and we move right in."

"But what if it doesn't work out?" As much as she hated to say it, she'd had enough experience to draw on. Things always looked great in the first few months, then they'd go downhill. She wasn't getting on that roller coaster again without being very sure.

"Of course it will," Mac said.

"Didn't you say that shifter lions don't just have one mate?" she asked.

"I said in some prides people have multiple partners. But my father doesn't, and I don't want that either. Guess I should've kept my mouth shut about that."

"Let's give it a bit more time." As much as she wanted to say yes, she had to be sure. Not only that, but she had to find a way to tell him the truth. Otherwise, they'd have a lie between them.

"How much time, Zora? Don't you trust me?"

"I do, but I need to feel that it's right."

"It is right," he insisted. "I'm sure of it."

"Please, Mac." For some reason he wanted her to decide right away. What was he afraid of? "This is a big decision for us both and we shouldn't rush it."

He didn't reply, instead he threw the stick away and kicked a rock.

"By the way, the new bookkeeper is going to meet with you on Friday," she said, eager to change the subject.

He groaned. "Before you started working for me I used to be buried in papers. Never realized how much I hated analyzing spreadsheets."

"Once everything's online, they'll be less intimidating."

"Intimidating?" Mac kicked another rock off the path. "I'm not intimidated by spreadsheets."

Perhaps that was the wrong word to use to an alpha male lion shifter. "What I meant was since spreadsheets aren't your thing, it's best to delegate that work. Then you can focus on what you do best."

"You can't always do what you want," Mac said.

"But don't you ever feel like you're going against your true nature?"

Mac stopped in his tracks. "What do you mean? You mean about having lots of partners? Zora, I told you, I'm not like that."

For a minute she wanted to smile. He was so concerned she'd think he wasn't serious about making a commitment. "I mean, you love cooking and you come up with great ideas. What's wrong with playing to your strengths?"

His expression softened. "I've had to do it all since I opened. It's been hard to let go of some things."

"You don't have to do it alone. Not anymore."

Mac was still staring at her, trying to figure out what her meaning was. "You're not bored working at the shop? You have an MBA, you could get a better job."

"I don't want to be stuck in a cube someplace in a corporate office. It's fun working at the coffee bar with you."

"Good answer. But it's not always that easy. Family likes to butt in." He put his arm around her.

Zora could sympathize with that. Butting in was what her sister, Diane did best. Their parents had left California and were living in Colorado now, so Zora didn't get to see them as often. But they hadn't been happy when she announced she didn't want to go into the family business and become a vet. At least Diane lived up to their expectations.

"Hey, let's go grab some beers and sit out on the patio. Might as well enjoy the rest of our afternoon off," Mac said.

Most of the houses in Bristol Hills had a pool in back, but Mac's didn't. Perhaps not surprising for a cat shifter. Instead he had a patio with a huge grill and outdoor kitchen.

"And after that?" she teased. "You never finished what you started upstairs."

"Don't worry about that, babe, I will."

3 Stay or Go

"Damn, I forgot I've got a meeting in the morning." Mac stretched out his long legs and extended his arms towards the headboard. "I'll skip it. I'd rather go check on the new store."

"What meeting?" Zora draped her arm across her pillow. "It wasn't on the schedule." It always amazed her how expert he was at multitasking. Only Mac could go from hot and heavy lovemaking to talking about a business meeting then back again.

Not surprisingly, their relaxing on the patio just lasted long enough for them to finish their beers. Then it was back to the bedroom.

"I didn't add it to the schedule. It's one of those business networking meetings where people drink burnt coffee and exchange business cards. With the new shop opening, maybe I should go and make nice."

"If you want, I can go," Zora said. "But that means I have to go home soon. I didn't bring anything to wear to a meeting."

"That's an excuse. I'll take you home, get your things and we'll come back."

From her position on her back, she darted her eyes over at him. Unfortunately, since he was propped up on the pillows she couldn't see his expression,

"It's late," she said.

"It's only 8:00."

"Mac, I've been here for hours. I'll go home and see you tomorrow."

"Why don't you want to stay?" he asked.

"I told you. I didn't bring anything to wear tomorrow. That includes underwear. And my toothbrush," she said.

Mac scooted down and propped himself up on his elbow so he could look at her. "Toothbrush? I've got extras in the bathroom cabinet. That's not it. You're still afraid of me."

"No. I told you that already." Even as she said it, she knew it wasn't entirely true.

"Remember when you started working at the shop, and I kept avoiding you?" he asked. "And you got mad at me? I had to do it. I was afraid of getting too close."

Those first few weeks had been stressful and totally aggravating. There she was, his assistant manager, and she'd had to rely on emails and texts to get answers from him.

"Mac, I just--"

"Let me finish." He caressed her cheek, and then rested his hand on her shoulder. "When I couldn't fight it anymore, I asked you to dinner. You know how hard that was? To admit I wanted to be with you? I didn't think I'd ever admit to needing anyone."

That dinner had been nice, though his discomfort had been obvious. Instead of displaying his usual confidence, he'd been tongue-tied and shy.

"You don't know how tough it was to tell you the truth," he said. "I was sure you'd quit, or just run away," Mac said, trailing his fingers across her breast. "But I had to honest. I wanted you to know the truth. I'm serious about this, Zora."

"Mac..." Her breath caught in her throat as he leaned over and took her nipple into his mouth. It drove her crazy when it did that. And he knew it.

Releasing her, he met her gaze. "Wash out your undies and wear that dress to the meeting. It looks great on you."

"It's not professional," she protested. "I'm going to a business meeting not a garden party." Seeing the desire in his hazel eyes, she felt her resolve melting away.

Ignoring her, he licked her nipple, alternating between licking and nipping.

"Okay you win," she said. "I'll stay." She ran her fingers over his chin, enjoying the feel of his prickly stubble. Instead of growing a full beard, he always left just enough on his face to tickle her skin.

Chuckling, he went back to sucking, then licking, then sucking.

"Mac! I said I'll stay," she gasped. At this point she didn't care what she wore to the meeting. How did he always get her to do what he wanted?

"Too late," he said, as he straddled her. "I win." Scooting down to the end of the bed, he quickly positioned himself to go after what he wanted.

Moaning, she arched her back as his lips made contact. Devouring her, he sucked and nipped. She knew his tongue was a regular human size when he wasn't shifting, but the way it felt she wondered if it was larger. Relentless, it continued to probe her sensitive spots, leaving her trembling. Raking his teeth against her clit, just enough to send her reeling, he followed it with a swipe of his tongue. Over and over until she cried out, begging him to take her before she exploded.

But he liked teasing her like this, stimulating her to the point of orgasm, then stopping. Gripping her thighs, he kept her legs apart, keeping her from trying to bring herself to release. Wet, hot juices dribbled from her as he continued his delicious torture.

"Mac, please," she whimpered. "Please..."

Bringing her to the point of orgasm yet again, he held back, ending his stimulation before she could come. Crying out in frustration, she pounded the bed with her fists.

"Relax, Zora. I'm not ready yet," he purred.

"Mac, I can't take much more!" she yelled. That would get his attention. "I want you!"

In no hurry to comply, he sat crouched, like a cat ready to spring. "I thought you liked foreplay." Lowering his head, he blew a puff of air on her engorged clit. That alone almost sent her through the roof.

"Mac! It's not supposed to go on forever!" she snapped, digging her fingers into the sheets.

"Cats like to play with their food." Another puff of air, followed by another swipe of his tongue.

She propped herself up on her elbows and glared at him. "Not for this long!"

Grinning, he shook his head, and then went back to licking and sucking. All she knew was if he didn't give her what she wanted soon, she was going to lose her mind.

Knowing when to be insistent and when to be gentle, he knew exactly how to bring her to the point where she was complete jelly. Maybe she was crazy not to want to move in with him. Even if they didn't have sex like this all the time, just falling asleep in his arms every night would be worth it. Mac would never hurt her, or make her regret giving him her heart.

In spite of everything, they could make it work. She had to believe it, just as he did.

Bringing her to the brink again, he didn't stop this time. Instead he continued stimulating her until she cried out, her body stiff as she orgasmed. So focused on the waves of pleasure washing over her, she barely felt the bed moving as he shifted himself to enter her. But when he sheathed himself inside her, her body tensed, and she instinctively raised her legs, pressing her thighs against him.

Groaning, he thrust deep inside her, filling her. Bracing her hands on his shoulders, she kept eye contact with him, trying to read what he was feeling.

She gripped him, digging her nails into his back, losing herself in the sensation of his exertions and her release. Exhausted, she held on, meeting his thrusts, willing herself to keep up with him. Moaning, he trembled, vibrating against her and inside her.

"Mac," she whispered.

Throwing his head back, he cried out. Whatever he was trying to say was unintelligible. His eyes were closed, his mouth open as he formed words that she couldn't understand.

Zora had never seen him like this before, his face flushed with exertion, growling with each release of his breath, knowing she was there and not knowing at the same time.

Emotions raw, her body completely open to him, she was aware that she had nothing to fear. But still she wondered if there was a point where the beast would overpower the man.

He nipped her earlobe, his teeth gliding down along her neck and shoulder. Eyes still closed, he found her mouth, greedily sucking her lips. Moving with more immediacy, he thrust his tongue into her mouth.

Mac's sweat-covered body was slick against hers, and her hands slid as she gripped his taut arms. As he moved, she felt his muscles tense and flex. Pleasure and pain mixed together between her legs, making her ache to be released while she wanted him to keep going.

Another orgasm hit her and she began to sob. Her breath came in ragged bursts, and her head lolled on the pillow. Energy drained from her, making her feel like she was close to losing consciousness.

"Zora," he groaned. "Hold on, baby. Please..." His body jerked and shuddered, like he was fighting the orgasm that racked him from head to toe. Finally, he was still.

She wasn't sure how much time had passed before she was aware of her surroundings again. It could've been minutes or maybe hours. When she opened her eyes, Mac was lying next to her and she was covered with the sheet.

"Are you all right?" he asked, his voice low.

"Yes, I'm okay." Her hand trembled when she touched his face. "What about you?"

He captured her hand and brought it to his lips. "I'm sorry. I didn't mean to be so rough."

"You didn't hurt me."

He sighed. "Are you sure?"

"I'm sure."

"I've never let that happen before. Not with..." He flopped on his back.

"Not with a human?" she asked. Sure he could be intense sometimes, and she enjoyed it. But this was the first time he'd seemed so bothered by it.

"I should've held back."

She felt his stiffness; he was closing her out. "Mac, if you feel the way you do about me, why hold back? Besides, if we do it more often, then you won't have all that stress built up," she said, trying to lighten the mood.

"It's not funny, Zora. Maybe you were right. I should take you home tonight." He moved to sit up, and she grabbed his arm.

"No. I'm staying. Now let's get some rest."

Easing down, he settled with his back to her. Great. That's not exactly what she meant. Snuggling against him, she slid her arm around his waist.

"Good night," she said.

Instead of replying, he grasped her hand and entwined his fingers with hers.

Certainly not the way she'd expected the evening to end. Maybe in spite of his insistence that she move in, he had fears too.

4 HOLDING BACK

The next morning Mac slid out of bed at 5:00 a.m., leaving Zora curled up under the covers. After a quick shower, he padded downstairs to make coffee. He had no appetite for breakfast this morning. Sitting down at the counter, he cradled his cup in his hands and reflected on the night before.

As much as he wanted to believe Zora's assurances, he wasn't comfortable with what he'd done. Drawing out the foreplay had excited them both, but he hadn't expected his own desire to be so explosive. Maybe she was right, he had spent too much time holding it all in. But even though they'd been together for most of the afternoon, he had to be honest with himself. He had been holding back each time, not wanting to overpower her.

The rough and tumble sex he'd had on occasion with other shifters wasn't something he wanted to bring into this relationship. Those times he'd been driven purely by need, not by love or affection.

When he heard Zora on the stairs, he jumped up and poured the remains of his coffee into the sink. Facing her this morning was not going to be easy.

"Good morning," she said.

Turning, he was surprised to find her smiling at him. Not the greeting he'd expected. "Morning. Hungry? I can whip up something before we go."

"No, I'll get something at the meeting. They'll serve stuff besides coffee at that meeting right? Bagels? Toast?"

"They did last time," he replied. "We should go." He turned off the coffeemaker and headed over to retrieve their shoes. When he bent to grab her sandals, dizziness hit him, and he staggered. Shit, he should've had something to eat. Closing his eyes to get his bearings, he felt a light touch on his arm.

"What's wrong? Are you okay?" Zora asked.

"Don't fuss. I'm all right," he snapped as he pressed the heel of his hand against his forehead.

"Fine." She snatched the sandals out of his hand and dropped them on the floor.

"I didn't mean--"

"Mac, I'm tired and I don't need your attitude." Shoving her feet into her shoes, she bent down to adjust the straps. "I barely slept, but how would you know? Your back was turned the whole night."

"Zora, I'm not in the mood to argue." So now she was pissed at him. Just what he needed.

"Neither am I." She grabbed her small handbag from the table next to the couch. "Where's the meeting? I don't want to be late."

"The library." Now he felt totally stupid. Was there a way to clean this up before they left the house? He could say he was sorry, or that he was a jerk. Or he could just let it go and hope she got over it. Option three was the safest one right now.

"Fine." Striding past him she grabbed the door knob and pulled, but the door didn't open. "It's locked."

Without a word, he turned the lock and stood back. Zora opened the door and walked out, slamming it behind her.

Mac shoved his hands into his pockets, as he listened to her car start up. After it rolled across the gravel and headed away, he sighed. Better to let her be mad and get it out of her system. How did he end up being the bad guy?

All the way to the meeting, Zora replayed their conversation in her mind. Was he blaming her for what happened? Now it was her fault? Mac had sulked all night and had the nerve to snap at her on top of it.

Heading down the hill wasn't so bad. It was a bit of a twisty drive in parts, but nothing she couldn't handle in her compact car. Of course, all the traffic was in town, and once she got on the main road things were backed up. It was a little after 7:00, and going into rush hour.

Once she arrived, she had to admit that Mac hadn't been wrong about the meeting. It was overflowing with burnt coffee, donuts, bagels and about twenty or so business owners from the local community. It didn't hurt to meet as many of them as she could, but she was glad when the mingling ended and they sat down to hear the presentation.

While the speaker droned on, she was tempted to whip out her phone and see what was going on at the shop. Who was opening today? Gina. She could text her and make sure all was well. Last week one of the coffee machines had broken down at the worst time. Anything could pop up.

Luckily, the presentation wrapped up in less than an hour. Zora couldn't remember one word of it though. Her mind was still on her earlier disagreement with Mac.

As she was standing by the buffet table, fiddling with her phone, she felt a presence next to her.

"Did you like the presentation?" An older man with graying sideburns and wisps of hair across his head was standing next to her. "We didn't get a chance to meet. My name is Bob Davidson."

"Hello. I'm Zora Mason." She shook his outstretched hand. "Do you own a business in town, Mr. Davidson?"

"Yes, I own the deli at the other end of Main Street, by the city hall," he replied. "You know, I was wondering if you're related to the Masons who used to run the vet practice on Elm Road."

"They're my parents. They sold it to my sister and her husband." Even as she said it, she wondered if she'd admitted too much.

"Ah yes, I thought so. Bristol Hills is a small town in some ways, isn't it? Even though there's over 100,000 people living here. So, Dr. Hill is your sister? She's been to some meetings from time to time." He checked his watch. "I always stay too long at these things."

She smiled in response and took a sideways glance at her phone. "I'd better get going," she said. "It was nice to meet you."

"You work for Mac MacKinnon at his shop. That's what you said during the introductions, right?"

"Yes," she said. "Do you know him?"

"Oh yes. I know he's opening a new shop in a strip mall over in Hermosa. I've been wondering how he got the investors. Do you know?"

She wasn't getting the best feeling from Bob. "No, I don't know those details, Mr. Davidson. Look, I'm sorry, but I really have to get going."

"Ms. Mason, I suggest you be very careful dealing with him. There's been talk." He leaned closer. "I've lived here all my life. I know things about some people here and what they're covering up."

"What are you talking about? Mr. Davidson--"

"Mac is not what he pretends to be." He narrowed his eyes at her. "Now he's going to open another shop. He's going to bring more of his kind here. You think I'm crazy, but I've seen things."

She didn't know whether to be frightened or to laugh. He sounded like he was from an old horror movie. Either he did know something, or he was trying to get information. "I don't know what you're talking about. What things?"

"Ask your father. He knows. He saw them too." Davidson straightened up and smiled at a man who passed by. "That kind will kill you without thinking about it. You'd better be very careful."

Frozen to the spot, Zora watched as Bob strolled away. What did her father have to do with anything? Unless Bob was hinting that he knew her parents had helped the shifters. And if he knew that, he might also know that her sister and brother-in-law were doing the same thing.

After the meeting, Zora dropped by her apartment to change into her work "uniform" which was just khakis and a denim shirt. By the time she got to the shop it was mid-morning.

The coffee bar was filled with customers dropping in for their break. Having a location within walking distance of a corporate office park and the community college meant there was a constant stream of customers through the day. Mac was nowhere in sight, though.

Zora went straight back to the office to put her things away. Half-expecting to find him at the desk, she was a bit disappointed.

Now that her systems were in place, things were running a lot smoother. And with the new bookkeeper handling the accounting, that was one more thing off Mac's plate. But she had something else to think about, namely, Bob's warning.

There had always been talk of shifters around these parts, and to most people they were urban legends. Even if Bob told others about Mac, who would believe him?

"Hey, Zora. Mac's brother is out there." Gina walked into the office, wiping her hands on her dark blue apron. She'd only been an employee for a couple of months, but she was a quick learner and great with the customers.

"He is? Did Mac call? I thought he'd be here by now."

"Yeah, he did. He said his meeting was running late, but he'd be here soon," Gina replied.

"Okay, then. Tell him to come on back."

Gina had barely left the office when Chris barreled in, a grin plastered on his face.

"Hi again!" He gave her a peck on the cheek. "Figured I'd come by and apologize for giving you a hard time yesterday."

"Hey, Chris." Zora sat at the desk and motioned to the chair across from her. "Have a seat. Did Mac tell you to come here?"

"Nope. I stopped by to get a cup of coffee." Chris picked up a pen off the desk and fiddled with it. "Have you met anyone else in the family yet?"

"No one but you." She sat

"Mac's been keeping you a secret." Chris winked. "My Dad and Mom are cool, but some others, forget it."

"What do you mean?" Zora asked.

"When my Dad decided to only have one mate, that was a big deal. My mom being human really got the gossip going too." Chris flicked the pen. "Some prides stick to tradition. Co-wives, co-husbands. Really old school shit."

"Co-wives?" He was echoing what Mac had mentioned. "Is that the norm?"

"Nah. Not anymore. I'd say maybe a quarter of the prides still do that. But that's just what I heard. I don't know any of those people." Chris dropped the pen. "My Mom wanted to introduce me to "nice" women. But I said, no way, all they want to do is settle down."

"Chris, has Mac ever...has he ever been a co-husband?"

"Mac? You're joking." He chuckled. "He's been a nomad for years. Refused to start a pride or take over Dad's. Nope. He's not trying to settle down. I know that for a fact."

Then why was he pressuring her to move in? Maybe he only wanted something temporary until he found someone else. She was just filler until he found a shifter. "So he never dated a lot?"

"Sure he did. With...people like us. Only once he met a girl and she was...like you. But that ended before he went to college. Not sure what happened." He leaned his arm on the edge of the desk. "I like human women. So what's your sister's name? I'm not looking for anything permanent, just a little fun."

"Chris. You've got one minute to tell me why you came here."

Zora looked up to see Mac standing in the doorway glaring at his younger brother.

"I was apologizing for yesterday. Remember? When you threw me out?" Chris leaped out of his chair. "Oh, look at the time. I've got to run. I'm meeting Grandma for lunch."

"Then you'd better get going," Mac said. "Talk to you later."

"Yeah, sure. Bye, Zora!" Chris eased around his brother and left the office.

Instead of acknowledging him, Zora turned on the computer and swiveled her chair to face front. What was the point hearing what he had to say? Now she knew what his intentions really were.

"We have to talk," he said, as he sat down.

She continued to ignore him. From now on their relationship would be professional.

"Would you look at me at least?" Mac asked.

"Why? I wouldn't want to fuss." She pushed the computer mouse across the desk. "I'm busy right now."

"How did the meeting go?"

The meeting. She'd already forgotten. "I got a bunch of business cards. Probably the same ones you have already."

"Probably. Was that guy Davidson there? He acts like the coffee bar is competing with his business."

"He was there," she replied. "How well do you know him?"

"Not well." Mac picked up an invoice from the pile of papers and examined it.

"Doesn't seem like this shop should be in competition," she remarked. "He owns a deli."

"Yeah, I know. Doesn't stop him from giving me dirty looks when I see him."

"He's got a lot of friends," Zora said. Didn't it concern Mac what the other business people thought?

"Maybe. But, so do I." Mac shuffled the papers around, looking through them.

"But do you think Bob can make trouble?" she asked.

"Bob?" He grinned. "You two on a first name basis now? He's just a crank. Nobody listens to him."

"He's not too happy with you opening the new coffee bar in Hermosa."

"Davidson can't stop me." Mac picked up another paper and studied it. "He shoots off his mouth sometimes. Like my brother."

"I've got to look at the orders. Do you mind?"

"Zora, did Chris say anything?"

"Nothing I want to discuss right now. I'm busy."

"Then we'll talk about it later." Mac stood up and left the office.

Obviously he wasn't happy being ignored, but she wasn't in the mood to talk right now. She had work to do.

5   OVERPOWERED

That evening after closing Mac stayed behind. Frustrated, he busied himself with cleaning up the coffee pots and setting things up for the next day.

Working always helped him to direct his energies. Otherwise, the urge to shift would be overpowering. Of course, sex was another way to work off those urges. A very enjoyable way.

Trying to talk to Zora alone hadn't worked at all. To make matters worse, somehow she managed to leave the shop without him realizing it.

He finished cleaning one of the pots and threw his towel into the trash. Why couldn't Zora trust him? If only she'd just understand him better. He hadn't meant to snap at her this morning. His desire for her was overpowering, but at the same time he was afraid of his feelings for her.

Shit. They had to resolve this.

After closing the shop, instead of going home, he headed over to Zora's apartment. Located in a complex not far from Main Street, her apartment was a two-bedroom with a view overlooking the woods.

When he ran up the front steps, he was filled with anxiety. What if she turned him away? When he pressed her door buzzer there was silence, and then he heard her voice over the intercom.

"Yes?"

"It's Mac. Can I come in?"

Tapping his fingers on the metal plate, he waited for her response. Not sure what he'd do if she refused him, he was filled with dread.

The door buzzer sounded and the door unlocked, giving him entry to the building. Wasting no time, he ran up the stairs and didn't stop until he was in front of her door. Anxious to talk to her face-to-face, he by-passed the door knocker and banged with his fist.

The door opened and she stood there, still in her work clothing. "You don't have to knock the door down," she said.

"I want to talk to you."

When she stepped out of the way, he bounded in and stood in the middle of the living room. Her apartment was small but cozy with a grey couch across from the TV, and a dining table across the room.

Zora closed the door and faced him. "Yes?"

"What did my brother say today? Why are you so mad at me?"

"You can start by telling me why you barked at me this morning," she said. "Then we can talk about what your brother said."

"What did he say?" Mac asked.

"On top of it, you turned away from me last night." She perched her hands on her hips.

"I didn't do it on purpose!" What did she expect him to do?

Zora glared up at him. "Chris said you're not ready to settle down."

"My brother doesn't know what I want. I want to be with you." He reached for her, but she darted away.

"I don't believe you."

Mac followed her into the dining area. "No one knows me like you do."

"Then why snap at me?"

"I was wrong," he admitted. "Zora, I don't want to lose you. I was afraid you'd change your mind about being with me."

She tried to get past him, but he grasped her arms and held her. The flash in her eyes excited him, igniting a fire that could only be quenched once he was inside her body.

He pulled her into his embrace. "Forget what my brother said. He doesn't know what I feel for you."

Relaxing against him, she slid her arms around his neck. "What about those co-wives?" she asked.

Damn Chris and his big mouth. "Forget that. It has nothing to do with us. My parents aren't like that and neither am I."

Being with her gave him life, like he could overcome anything. If she left him, what would he have? He'd go back to being alone.

"Zora, I want you in my life." Mac tangled his fingers in her hair. "I want you for love, and business, and companionship. Do you want me?"

She smiled up at him. "What about sex?"

"Hell, yeah," he said.

With that she guided him to the couch and they sat down. Desperate to undress each other, Mac started unbuttoning her shirt just as Zora was unbuttoning his. He met her eyes and couldn't help but laugh as they sat there, tugging at each other's clothing.

"I knew I should've picked t-shirts for the coffee bar and not shirts with buttons," Mac said.

Zora pulled him closer for a kiss, letting her lips linger as her tongue teased his. It was maddening for her to draw it out like this. He enjoyed kissing her, but he was ready for more. But when he tried to turn the tables, and continue to undo her shirt, she grasped his hands.

"Not so fast," she breathed. "I thought you liked foreplay."

So this was payback, huh? She'd torture him the same way he'd done to her. Part of him wanted to experience it. Nothing like letting her caress and kiss him until he was ready to explode. But not tonight. As it was his body was aching for release, and he had to have her now.

"Tonight I'm in no mood to wait." Distracting her with a kiss, he quickly unbuttoned her shirt and slid his fingers under her bra.

Her soft moans encouraged him to explore her body. All that mattered now was proving to her that he was serious. She was the one he wanted, and she'd be the only one. Easing her down, he planted kisses as he freed her from her shirt.

Releasing her from the rest of her clothing was easy. He threw her pants across the room and chuckled as they landed on top of the TV.

"Mac!' She sat up and pointed at the television. "Take them down."

"No," he said, leaning down to plant a kiss above her belly button. "I'm busy." Fighting back his hunger, he fingered the soft folds between her legs. The musky, sweet scent of her arousal filled his nostrils, so strong he could taste it.

She moaned and whispered his name. In response, he eased two fingers into her, feeling her juicy wetness. Did she realize what she was doing to him? Even though he ached to take her and fill her with everything he had, he had to hold back and not let the predator out. Not again.

Zora wasn't prey or some helpless victim, she trusted him. No matter how strong his urges were, he had to keep them under control.

"What's wrong?" she asked. She was staring at him, her expression unsure. A light sheen of sweat covered her brown skin, reminding him of how she'd looked when she'd come out of the shower.

"Huh?" His thoughts had taken him far away from her, and she'd sensed it. "Let's go to bed. It'll be more comfortable."

Mac helped her to her feet and walked hand-in-hand with her to the bedroom. Once inside, she turned on the lamp, pulled back the covers and climbed into bed.

"Are you sure you're okay?" she asked, watching him expectantly.

"Sure." It only took seconds for him to undress and join her. Losing himself in a mind-blowing kiss, he felt his tension evaporating. It would be okay. There was nothing to worry about.

Rolling onto his back, he gripped her hips as she straddled him. Throwing her head back, she squeezed her breasts, playing with them as he would've. Watching her, his desire scorched him like fire, pushing him to the edge of his endurance.

Groaning, he squeezed her hips and tried to get her to lower herself on top of him. But she resisted him and continued to caress herself. Then, without warning, she reached down and took his cock in her hands, teasing the tip with her thumb.

If only she knew how hard he was fighting to hold on. Fear gripped him, as a voice in his head amplified his anxieties. You'll hurt her and she'll hate you. She'll hate you if she sees what you really are.

An urge ripped through him, and he grabbed her and flopped her onto her back. Positioning himself, he grunted as he prepared to enter her moist center.

Inside him the beast urged him on, encouraging him to take her now, to find release and not care how he did it. While the man cried out, resisting the raw need and desiring to join with her, feel her love and her acceptance.

Struggling against himself, he moaned in anguish as he felt his erection dissipating. Barely able to enter her, he made a half-hearted attempt. By now she realized what was happening, and she held him as he rocked against her. He was able to relieve himself, though he knew she hadn't gotten much out of it.

Spent and ashamed, he buried his head in the crook of her neck, not wanting to see her expression.

Stroking the back of his head, she murmured his name. "Mac, it's all right."

Her assurances shamed him; it wasn't all right. This had never happened to him before. What was she thinking of him? Easing out of her embrace, he plopped down next to her, his face turned away.

"Don't shut me out again." Zora touched his cheek, forcing him to look at her. "You're stressed. It happens."

"Not to me." He tried to turn away again, but her grip held him.

"You need to rest. You've been driving yourself too hard," she said.

There had to be a way to work this out. But would Zora still be there?

6 PRACTICING TO DECEIVE

Another morning and another sleepless night. Zora stood out on her tiny balcony, going over the events of the night before. Yet again Mac was keeping things bottled up and closing himself off. She'd have to get him to talk to her. Otherwise, they wouldn't be able to move forward.

Sipping her coffee, she looked out over the woods, which were still shrouded in early morning mist. With all his complaining about her not staying over at his house, Mac had left her place only a couple of hours after arriving. It didn't make any sense that he'd be ashamed about what happened. She knew what a passionate lover he was; he had nothing to prove to her.

She went back inside and checked her phone. 7:00 a.m. Time to get going. Mac would probably be at the coffee bar, just as he always was at this hour. No amount of persuasion could get him to slack off just a little bit. Even with five other people helping him run the shop, he still acted like he had to do it all.

Well, at least she could get more coffee once she got to work. Zora emptied her cup into the kitchen sink, grabbed her handbag and headed out.

In spite of the traffic, she pulled into the back parking lot within minutes. Letting herself in through the rear service door, she heard music and conversation from the shop. Mac's apron was still hanging from the closet door. Strange. He should've been here by now.

The back door swung open and Mike, one of the baristas, ran in. When he saw her, he stopped short. "Hey, Zora, did Mac call you? He texted me to come this morning and cover for him."

"No, he didn't. Maybe he had to go to the other location." A pang of fear hit her. What if something had happened to him? Mac had been so down when he'd left the apartment last night.

"He said he had an appointment. Who's out front?" Mike rolled up his sleeves and disappeared into the closet.

"Just got here myself. Zora went to the doorway and glanced around the shop. Customers were milling around the case where the breakfast rolls and buns were displayed. The aroma of freshly brewed coffee wafted in the air, along with smells of cinnamon. Gina and Jennifer, the other barista, were busy serving coffee and ringing up purchases.

Mike slipped past her and joined the others behind the counter. Why didn't Mac call her? She wasn't just his assistant, she was his girlfriend, damn it.

Just a couple of days ago he'd been pressuring her to move in and now he was barely communicating. Whatever he was keeping bottled up had to come out.

"Mac, I didn't expect to see you back here so soon."

"Glad you could see me on short notice, Diane." He sat down across from his vet, Dr. Diane Hill. One of the things he liked about her was that she kept extended office hours for her special patients. She even had a separate entrance so they could have their privacy.

And there was almost nothing more important to a shifter than discretion. Otherwise, the Bob Davidson's of the world would have all the proof they needed that shifters did exist.

"So what's the problem?" Diane asked. Behind her was a huge case filled with books with dark binders. Everything was neat and orderly. Usually Mac met her in one of the exam rooms, but this wasn't that type of visit, so they were in her private office.

How to describe it without sounding like a total idiot? He'd been coming to her for years, and she'd heard just about everything. But this was not going to be easy to talk about.

"Well, I had another problem...like the one we talked about the other day."

"I don't see that it was a problem, Mac. You have been working very hard and sometimes letting off a bit of stress is called for," Diane explained, her voice soft and comforting. "We discussed this several months ago, remember? If you hold back too much, it'll make things worse. Just set aside time to shift. That's who you are. You can't fight it." She folded her hands, revealing neat unpolished nails.

"Yes, but last night I had an opposite problem. I...I was with someone and I...it..." This totally sucked. Might as well come out with it. "I couldn't perform."

Her expression remained mild, though he did detect a slight lift of her eyebrow. Was she laughing at him but afraid to show it? The great and powerful lion shifter who couldn't get it up.

"Mac, I'm sure it's related to what we discussed. A build up of stress. You've got the new place opening, and you're in this relationship. As long as I've known you, you've never mentioned a girlfriend." Diane opened up a folder and looked through the contents. "There's a lot going on."

"I know." He crossed his legs and tried to get comfortable. "Usually, work helps me hold off my urge to shift."

"That's not a good idea. I told you that last time. Balance is better." She pulled a pen out of the pocket of her crisp, white jacket and scribbled something down. "We just did a check up, so I don't see a need for another one."

"Are you sure? Maybe I need a prescription?"

Diane frowned, and pushed a lock of her shoulder-length brown hair off her face. "You're a healthy male. Besides, you have no idea how human medications will affect you. So don't do anything on your own, okay?"

"Okay." She was right. There was nothing wrong with him physically. "So, do you mind if I ask you a personal question."

"Sure," she replied.

"Do you think a human woman would be able to meet the demands of...of sex with me?" His heart thundered in his chest. This was so damned awkward. Diane had seen him practically from every angle, so there no reason to be shy with her. Though she was about the same age he was, most times she came across as older and more reserved.

"Oh, she's not a shifter. You didn't mention that last time." Diane gently tapped her pen against her temple. "But you told me your mother isn't a shifter. I'm not sure why you're concerned. Has she ever had any problems?" The last thing he wanted to do was have a discussion about his parents and sex. "Not that I'm aware of."

"Then in my opinion, if your girlfriend is aroused and understands that your needs may be more intense than the average human male, then you both should be in tune."

"Oh, we're in tune all right."

"Mac, human women are not the weaker sex, no matter what you may have heard." She smiled. "You may have more stamina and power to draw on, but frankly I don't see that as a disadvantage." Diane cleared her throat as she dropped her pen and closed the folder.

If he wasn't sure, he'd think she was a bit embarrassed. Well, it wasn't like they discussed sex all the time. Diane was personable, but she always stayed professional, which is why he trusted her opinion.

"That means it'll be okay between us?" A weight fell off his shoulders and he was more at ease than he'd felt in a while. Zora had never shown him anything but love and acceptance. He'd worked himself up over nothing.

"Certainly, Mac. The more you hold back the more pressure and anxiety build up. If she accepts you as you are, what do you have to fear? Just keep communicating."

Communicating. The one thing he hadn't been doing over the past couple of days. It was hard, but he'd have to make the effort. Anything to keep Zora in his life.

"So where did you meet her? Is she from here?" Diane asked.

"Yeah. But she moved to the East Coast for a while. She came back here to go to business school. She works at my coffee bar."

"Oh, working with someone and having a relationship with them can be challenging. Just ask my husband." She smiled. "So, this sounds serious."

"It is."

"Have you discussed mating with her?"

"Not in so many words," he replied. "I'm waiting to bring that up." No need to overwhelm her with things like mating and other shifter stuff. Not yet, anyway.

"I see." Diane tapped her fingers on the desktop. "If she's from town, I might know her family. What's her name?"

"Zora Mason. She said her folks moved away, so I don't know if she has anyone here," Mac replied.

"Zora Mason?" Diane's light brown eyes grew wide. As she came to her feet, she gripped the edge of the desk. Though she was probably about 5' tall, she suddenly seemed much more imposing.

"Yeah. She's been working at the shop for about four months. Something wrong?"

"I...um...I forgot an appointment, Mac. I'm so sorry. Was there anything else? I hope I answered your questions..." Her voice trailed off, like she was distracted.

"I feel better already." He stood and extended his hand. "See you later."

Diane grasped his hand and shook it. "Yes, Mac, you probably will be."

"Huh?"

"For coffee." Her expression brightened and she smiled again, but it seemed forced. "I've been meaning to stop by the shop, but I didn't want to intrude on your privacy."

"Coffee's on me. Tell them you're a friend." No doubt Zora and the others were holding things down at the coffee bar. He'd go by the new location and see how the work was coming along. "See you!" Mac waved and headed back out the private entrance, which was actually a back door that led directly to the parking lot.

Walking out into the bright sunshine, he felt the tension leaving him. Everything was fine. He had nothing to worry about. Quickening his pace, he almost felt like jumping into his convertible instead of opening the door. Zora had been right. He'd been working too hard. Not only that, he had let his fears get the best of him. Everything would be great from now on.

7   SISTER TO SISTER

Lunchtime at the coffee bar and Mac still hadn't arrived. Zora finished with the customer she was ringing up, and headed to the back office. Maybe he'd texted her.

She grabbed the phone and swiped the screen. No text messages, no calls. Was he okay? It wasn't like him to disappear like this. Why text Mike and not her?

"Zora?" Jennifer leaned into the doorway. "There's someone who wants to see you."

"Something wrong?" On rare occasions a customer wanted to talk to a manager, and when that happened, she did everything to solve their problem.

"No. It's somebody who knows Mac," she replied. "Can I tell her you'll be out in a minute?"

"Sure. I'll be right there." Zora checked the phone one more time. Maybe she was getting worked up over nothing.

As soon as she saw who it was, Zora knew she was in trouble. Standing off to the side, between the espresso maker and the dessert display was her sister, Diane. For a minute she wondered if she should dart back into the office and lock the door after her. That had worked when she and her sister had gotten into scrapes as children. But just like back then, sooner or later she had to come out and face the music.

"Hi, Diane."

"Is that all you're going to say?"

This was not the place for a blow out, and goodness knows they'd had their share.

"Let's go over there. I won't be long." Diane pointed to a table by the front window.

Maybe staying out here would be better. They'd both be less likely to yell if they had an audience. Zora followed her sister and sat in the overstuffed chair opposite her.

"Mac came to see me this morning and we got to talking. Imagine my surprise when he told me who his girlfriend was." Diane set her handbag down on the table between them. "Why didn't you tell me? Now I know why you lied whenever I asked about your new job."

"I didn't lie. I said it was a small company on Main Street."

"You never gave me a straight answer. And you're dating him? Are you insane?" Diane glanced around her.

"When I came here and he had a job opening. I don't have to check in with you."

"But you forgot one important thing. I know you were in my desk drawer. You were supposed to be helping me set things up on the computer, and instead you were rifling through the private files."

"I was not riffling--I had to look for information." Unfortunately, she knew her denial wasn't very convincing. Those files were kept locked up in a drawer of her sister's desk. Diane would've taken the key with her if she'd known what Zora would do once she'd left the office.

"Liar!" Diane gripped her handbag, digging her fingers into the leather. "I trusted you. You've compromised me, don't you see? Our patients have to be able to trust me and Michael."

When she'd volunteered to help her sister set up some of her business records online, Zora had never expected to find out the truth about her special patients. She'd always suspected that the people who used the side entrance--and never brought any animals--had some other reason for being at the clinic.

Seeing how all her other records were accessible to the office staff, Zora hadn't understood why Diane would keep those old folders separate. Once she saw Mac visit the clinic a couple of times, it was all the motivation she needed to prove if her theory was correct.

"So, you and Mom and Dad knew all this time about--" Zora lowered her voice to a whisper. "Shifters and you never told me? Talk about trust."

"Shhhhh!" Diane gripped her bag harder. "As long as people think they're just urban legends, nobody really cares. I don't need you messing things up."

"Mess things up? I'm not a kid anymore. Besides, I needed to know if those files were related to the business. You asked for my help and I needed access to everything."

"Why? I told you what you needed to know."

"You asked for my help, remember? You didn't respect or trust me enough to tell me what you were doing?"

"That's beside the point. Mac's going to wonder why I didn't tell him we're sisters."

"So why didn't you?"

Diane pursed her lips so hard she looked like her head was going to explode. "Because that was your job. You should've been honest and told him who you were. You didn't take this job because you wanted it. You only came here to check him out. Isn't that why you asked about him the day he visited the clinic? The day I told you to mind your business--remember that day?"

Zora was about to reply when Gina brought a large cup of coffee to the table. She set it down and placed a spoon next to it. "Here you go, Dr. Hill. Hope you like it. By the way, my dog is doing so much better now. He's running around like crazy."

Diane smiled. "Thank you, Gina. So glad to hear that. This coffee smells great."

Gina smiled and wiped her hands on her apron. "It's a little extra caramel. Or maybe I shouldn't say that with my manager here."

"Don't worry about her. She's a big rule breaker herself." Diane stirred the whipped cream into her beverage.

"Yes, I've been told that all my life," Zora replied.

Once Gina walked away, Diane's smile disappeared. "I don't know what you're playing at, but this has to stop. You're going to give your notice and break it off with Mac. He doesn't need to be dragged into your games."

Was she kidding? Her sister was acting like they were both teenagers again fighting over high school nonsense. "I like this job, Diane. There's an opportunity for me to help him with the business."

Diane shot her a skeptical look. "Since when are you excited about that? You were always complaining that Mom and Dad talked you into going back to school. They even helped you pay for it."

"Yes, they helped me, and I appreciate it. I'm glad about it now." She hadn't expected to like going to business school of all things.

"And now you're a serious business woman? Right," Diane snorted. "You came here to check him out. It was just by luck that he had a job opening."

"I admit it. I was wrong to do what I did. Haven't you ever done anything silly?" Zora asked, already knowing the answer.

"No. I studied hard and got good grades. I didn't have time for silliness," Diane replied. "It's about time you grew up."

They'd had this conversation before, and Zora was tired of it. "If I'm so terrible, you should've told Mac to fire me. Now, I know I was wrong and I'm going to let him know we're related. But I'm not quitting and I'm not breaking up with him."

Zora tensed as she noticed a man at the next table look up from his paper. Though with the pop music playing in the background, and the sounds of conversations and hot milk hissing in the cappuccino machine, it wasn't likely he could make out what they were saying.

"I didn't come here to argue," Diane said.

"Yes you did. And you wanted to do it out here so the staff could see you admonishing your irresponsible little sister."

Diane's mouth fell open as she put her cup down. "I did not. Mac invited me to come and have a cup of coffee on him."

"You came to confront and embarrass me. But it won't work."

"I'm concerned about my reputation and the well-being of my patients. Mac is not used to letting people get close."

"That's funny because someone else told me that recently. Ever heard of Bob Davidson?"

"Yes. Dad knows him."

"He said he and Dad saw something. Do you know about that?"

"Bob had an accident and he hit an animal, or so he thought. Dad told me when he got to the scene he realized something wasn't right. That's how he found out shifters were real."

"Then what?"

"That's all I know about it," Diane protested. "No one listens to Bob Davidson anyway." She gulped down the rest of her coffee. "I've got to go. I'm late for an appointment."

"And I've got to get back to work."

"Wait a minute. What are your feelings for Mac?"

"Why do you want to know?" Zora asked.

"He works hard to make a good life for himself and he doesn't need someone who's going to hurt him. You've been in and out of love since we were kids. I've watched you jump from one thing to another without sticking with anything."

"Don't scold me, Diane. I'm not thirteen, I'm thirty. I know what I want now."

"That's what you said when you moved East to go to that fashion school. Then you quit and got a job in a boutique. Then you were designing websites. I'm shocked you actually finished school and got your MBA."

Zora had always known what Diane thought of her. Even when she'd worked with her sister in the clinic, their relationship had been more formal than friendly. But this was too much. She was a grown woman. Why did she have to prove anything to anybody in the first place?

Her heart was thumping as the fight or flight response kicked in. She had to get out of here now before she embarrassed herself in front of the customers. "I'm done here." Zora jumped up and pushed the table so she could get out from behind it, but Diane grabbed her wrist.

"Mac cares about you, and he won't understand if you decide to flit away next week. He wants a mate, not a friend with benefits."

Zora snatched her arm away. Managing not to bump into anyone, she wound her way through the maze of tables and rushed into the back office. Shutting the door behind her, she pressed herself against it in case Diane tried to barge in.

Now she remembered why she'd been happy to move across the country. She didn't go into the family business. She didn't marry the first guy she had sex with. She didn't want to live a safe, quiet, boring life.

How dare Diane insist that she break up with Mac? Yet again, her sister was trying to run her life and she wasn't putting up with it. She was in love with him.

But could they really make it work? And once she told him that Diane was her sister, would he understand her deception? If not, he might shut her out forever.

8 MAKE UP TO BREAK UP

It wasn't until 3:00 that afternoon that Mac finally called the shop to check in. Still pissed from her argument with her sister, Zora didn't hide her annoyance when Gina told her that Mac was on the phone.

She went to the back office to take the call. "Mac where have you been all day?" she asked, as she perched on the edge of the desk.

"Over at the other location. A part didn't come in and I had to chase after the vendor."

"You should've let me know. I'm your assistant manager, remember?"

"Sorry about that, babe. Next time I'll follow procedures and call you first. Look, I've still got some things to do over here. I'll pick you up from your place later, okay?"

"Mac, we have to talk."

"Yeah, we'll talk. Throw some things in a bag and I'll pick you up. We'll have dinner at my place...and breakfast too. Okay?'

"Okay," she said.

"You don't sound too happy."

"I am."

"Great. I'll see you later."

As she hung up the phone, she felt like she'd been kicked in the stomach. He sounded so upbeat. That would probably change once they had their talk. If it went anything like her conversation with Diane, she doubted she'd still be there for breakfast.

That evening, Zora was at a loss for conversation as they drove to his house. Instead she listened as he described what was going on at the new shop. Unable to control his excitement, he went over every detail of the construction as though he'd never told her about it before. Normally, his enthusiasm would've been contagious, but her thoughts were a million miles away.

Once they got to his house, Mac went straight to the outdoor grill, leaving her to toss the salad. Determined to tell him after dinner, she went over the conversation in her mind. Of course he'd understand. They both might even laugh about it.

Unfortunately, by the time they'd finished dinner and loaded the dishwasher, she'd lost her enthusiasm for bringing the subject up. They were having such a nice evening. Why mess things up?

"Am I boring you about the new shop?" Mac asked, as he offered her a beer from the fridge. "I've been talking about it all evening."

"Not at all, Mac. You know I love to talk about business." She took the bottle and settled herself on one of the chairs by the counter.

He grinned, and then took a swig of his beer. "You're part of it too. I know you want to talk about what happened the other night. It won't happen again. Things will be fine from now on." Mac came from around the counter and slid his arm across her shoulders.

"That's why you went to see...your doctor today?" she asked. He'd been so worried he'd gone straight to the doctor. That's how concerned he'd been that he couldn't satisfy her. Everything he'd done had only shown her how much he wanted her in his life. She couldn't throw that away by letting him know that he couldn't trust her.

"Yeah, did Dr. Hill stop by the shop? I told her to come by and have a coffee on me." He kissed her cheek.

"Dr. Hill? Um, yeah, she came by." Zora hoped he didn't hear the hesitation in her voice. "Are you feeling okay?"

"Sure I am. Babe, I meant to make things up to you tonight. But it's been a long day. Let's get comfortable." He chuckled. "There's a game on."

"You're going to watch the game instead of work? I'm shocked." "No work tonight, babe. It's just us relaxing in front of the TV." Mac dropped down on the cushions and stretched his legs out. "By the way, before you sit down, could you grab my beer? I left it on the counter. Why are you giving me that look?"

Men. Zora got the beer and handed it to him. "Anything else? A backrub? How about a sandwich?"

"You can save the backrub for later. Or maybe you can rub something else," he teased.

"Or maybe you can." She sat next to him.

"Oh, I can. And you'll love it." He turned the TV on. "But first things first. It's game time." Resting a hand on her thigh, he took another gulp of beer.

Instead of taking out his tablet and working, he wanted to sit here and relax with her in front of the TV. He certainly seemed happier. Maybe it wasn't the right time for a serious talk.

"Tomorrow I've got to go drop in on my grandmother. She left me a message," Mac said. "I'll head over to her place after we open the shop."

"Just dropping by for a visit?"

"My brother's just stirring shit up. She wants to talk to me about it. I'll go straighten him out."

Looked like she wasn't the only one with sibling troubles. Obviously Mac and Chris had a few issues to work through.

Later that night, she was in bed with Mac's strong arms around her. It was like being wrapped in a warm, cocoon with his body spooned against hers. But in spite of the comfort, she wasn't able to sleep. No matter how much she avoided it, she'd have to tell him the truth.

Mac wasn't like Diane; he wouldn't think badly of her. But as much as she tried to convince herself of that, she dreaded losing his trust. She'd have to take the risk though, and stop hiding.

And she did want to move forward with their relationship, just as he'd asked her to. She'd tell him tomorrow night after dinner.

9 FAMILY BUSINESS

As Mac pulled into his grandmother's driveway, he prepared for another clash with his brother. Everything was going so great now. His relationship with Zora was getting better, his new shop was about to open, and he finally felt confident about the future. He didn't need family troubles getting in the way. Not now.

He rang the bell and only had to wait a few seconds before the door opened. Lena stood in the doorway, her brown eyes shining. Whenever he mentioned his grandmother, his human acquaintances always pictured someone very mature and stately. But they'd never met a lion shifter version of a grandma.

"Come in, stranger," she said. "It's about time." Though she was always active in human form, biking, playing tennis, running, most people had no idea that her athletic body was mostly due to her activities in lion form.

As the female head of the family, she was the one everyone came to. Whether they were lions or not, they looked for her counsel (and in some cases, approval) before doing anything within the shifter community.

The funny thing was, Lena was, for all her influence, the one who probably cared the least about protocol. But her wisdom and status as senior female in the MacKinnon pride made her the unofficial leader of the group of lion shifters that lived in the town of Hermosa. Out of the population of 55,000 or so inhabitants, at least 1/4 of the people could trace their origins to a shifter ancestor.

"Hi Grandma." Mac kissed her cheek before kicking off his shoes. "How have you been?"

"If you'd stop by more often, you'd know." She gathered her shoulder-length silvery hair into a ponytail. "I'm only about a half hour away."

Lena was wearing a long, sleeveless dress decorated with flowers, similar to the one Zora had worn the other day. He'd have to bring the two of them together at some point. Lena was the one he could always go to. In fact, he needed them to get to know each other and, more importantly, to get along.

"Yeah, I know." He gathered her into his arms for a hug. "Don't be too hard on me. I've been busy getting the new shop ready."

She playfully swatted at him. "From what Chris tells me, you're busy with something else too. Come, let's go have some coffee."

Of course his brother would be running his big mouth. "Where is Chris?" Mac followed her into the large sunny kitchen. Windows rimmed the sink area, giving a view of the back yard and the neighbor's house across the way.

"Down the street. You remember the Grants? You dated one of the daughters. Or was it all three of them?" Lena rolled her eyes and took two coffee mugs off the shelf. "Well, the youngest boy restored an old sports car. Chris has been drooling over it."

"I didn't date all of them at once, Grandma. I tried to, though." Mac sat at the wide granite-topped counter. Living with his grandmother during his college years had been great. He'd had none of the lectures about responsibility that his father liked to give him every other week. The only down side was that Lena had noticed everything.

She'd given him a lot of leeway, but she had no problem putting her foot down. Once he'd gotten his teenage rebellion out of the way--something that had lasted well into his twenties--he could finally appreciate her firmness with him.

Lena smiled and got the coffee pot from the burner. "I almost gave up on your settling down. Once you started that business, all you did was work. I'm glad you have someone now."

"What did Chris tell you?"

"I'd rather you tell me. Your brother likes to embellish."

"She's not a shifter, Grandma." Mac waited for her response.

"Like the girl you dated in high school. The one you told me about." Lena poured his coffee, and then filled her own cup. "But I thought it didn't work out because she was human."

Mac picked up his spoon and swirled it around the cup. "I didn't feel comfortable telling her I was a shifter. It got hard to hold it in. She figured out I was hiding something from her and she got tired of it."

"And this relationship is going to be different?"

"It already is," he replied. "That's why I told her I was a shifter. I know I can trust her."

"Okay." Lena set the cream and sugar in front of him. "So tell me about her."

"Wait, in your message you said you wanted to talk about Dad." Maybe he could delay this conversation a bit.

"We'll talk about your father later. Drink your coffee and give me the details."

"I've been seeing her for three months. I met her when she applied for the assistant manager job at my shop."

Lena sipped her black coffee. She never took anything extra, and couldn't understand why anyone would add any of the toppings and syrups that Mac's customers loved having in their beverages.

"How long did you know her before you asked her out?"

"Three weeks."

She chuckled. "Longer than I would've guessed. Why did you wait?"

"Grandma, humans are different. Shifters act on instinct." He'd known right after meeting her that he wanted to know Zora better. It was either right or it wasn't.

"Humans act on instinct too, though it doesn't work for them as well as it does for us," she pointed out. "So, she knows what you are?"

"Yes. I told her and it's okay."

Lena looked skeptical. "She's not one of those people, is she? The ones who have a sex thing for shifters. I've dealt with a few of those."

"Have you? In what way?" Trying to hide his amusement, he purposely didn't meet her eyes. One thing she wasn't shy about was talking about sex. But then, not many shifters were. It was just a natural part of living and mating.

"You are the only one who could get away with asking me that, Mackenzie. And it's none of your business." Lena smirked. "But really, are you sure she's all right with it?"

"She's more than all right with it. I asked her to move in."

"I see. So this is it, then," Lena said. "You've chosen a human as a mate. Just like your father."

"If she agrees, yes." It was only a matter of time before she said yes. There wasn't a doubt in his mind that they belonged together.

"Mackenzie, I wonder if she really understands what you're asking her to do. Is she from this area?"

"Yeah, she's from Bristol Hills. People around here are used to hearing about shifters," Mac replied.

"But there's a difference between hearing stories and actually being in a relationship with one," Lena remarked. "Did you tell her that you want to mate with her?" She sipped her coffee, her gaze fixed on him.

Whenever she gave him that no bullshit look, Mac knew he couldn't hide anything. "Not in so many words...but I wouldn't ask her to move in if I wasn't serious." Once she moved into the house, he'd bring up the part about becoming his mate. They'd take it a step at a time.

"Don't you think she should know your plan beforehand? She'll become a member of our pride once she's mated."

Not that he hadn't thought of that, but the way his grandmother said it made it sound ominous. "Of course she will. That won't be a problem."

"She'll have to be introduced into our family, though, and into the community," she replied.

"Grandma, mom is human. It's not a big deal if I mate with one."

"Your mother had to adjust to being in our world, Mackenzie. She made sacrifices. You have to be sure that the woman you love is up to the challenge." Lena picked up her spoon and absently tapped it on the counter. "She grew up in Bristol Hills? What's her family name?"

"Her name is Zora Mason. I haven't met her parents yet. They live in Colorado."

"Mason? Hmmm...Mason. I wonder if she's related to Dr. Mason. You know him."

"Dr. Mason?" The name sounded vaguely familiar, but he couldn't place it.

"Of course. I took you to him once...no that was Chris. Years ago when your parents sent both of you here for the summer."

He didn't remember that summer at all or Dr. Mason. "Thousands of people live in Bristol Hills, Grandma. I'm sure there are lots people named Mason," he protested.

"I'm sure there are, but you know who I'm talking about. His daughter has a vet practice over there, doesn't she?" Lena motioned towards him, using her spoon for emphasis. "Yes, that's right. Dr. Mason turned his practice over to her before he and his wife moved to Denver. Isn't that your vet?"

"Yeah, I go to Dr. Hill. So?"

"Dr. Mason had two daughters. I met him at a birthday party just before he moved. It was for...let me see...was that Charlie Sanchez or was it his brother--"

Mac gulped his coffee and waited for his grandmother to go through the degrees of separation between Dr. Mason and whoever had the party. There was no use interrupting her, she'd just start all over again if he did.

"No, it was Charlie all right. He invited Dr. Mason and his wife. That's where it was. We were talking and I reminded him that I'd brought you to his clinic--"

"It wasn't me, it was Chris. Remember?"

"Just you wait until you're my age." Lena grinned. "And don't interrupt me." She cradled her cup between her hands. "Anyway, Dr. Mason mentioned his girls when we were talking. He said the youngest one didn't have an interest in going to med school. She wanted to do something in fashion or whatever," she said. "He wasn't happy about it. But I told him that children will figure things out on their own."

Fashion? That's what Zora had mentioned she'd tried for a while. But how could it be? Now that Lena mentioned it, there was a slight resemblance between Zora and Dr. Hill, but nothing that jumped out at him. Not to mention that his doctor was reserved and a bit stiff. Zora was outgoing and certainly a lot of fun to be around. They couldn't possibly be sisters.

"I don't know, Grandma. Seems like Dr. Hill would've mentioned it. I told her who I was seeing." But thinking back on their conversation, her demeanor had changed when she'd heard Zora's name.

"Your aunt's staying with me again for the winter. She might know." Lena tapped her fingers on the counter. "Lily! Come here for a minute!"

"What is it?"

Mac turned to see his Aunt Lillian enter the doorway. She and Lena were fraternal twins. Since Mac had never met his great-grandparents, he wasn't sure who looked like whom. Unlike her twin sister Lena, Lillian kept her hair its original brown, and her build was shorter and stockier.

"Mac! Nice to see you." Lily waved. "I'm on my way out, Lena. What is it?"

"Tennis again? That good-looking tennis teacher must be working overtime," Lena said. "And I thought you came here every year to get away from the snow."

"It's not tennis today. I'm going running in the hills. We've got a group together." She perched her hands on her rounded hips. "I'm in a hurry. What do you want?"

"You remember, Dr. Mason? He had two daughters right?" Lena asked.

"Of course I know him. One of them is a vet in Bristol Hills where Mac lives. I heard the other one was in New York City for a while, but she moved back here a few years ago."

"How do you know that, Aunt Lillian?" Mac asked. "You're only in California for a couple of months a year. How do you know about Dr. Mason?"

Lily rolled her eyes. "Everyone knows Dr. Mason, Mac. He's friends with Dr. Green. Dr. Green has a clinic in Denver, and when Cousin Stanley went there for foot surgery, they got to talking."

Mac couldn't believe what he was hearing. Who the hell was Dr. Green and what did Cousin Stanley have to do with anything? "What?"

"Last summer Cousin Stanley came to my house for lunch and he told me about Dr. Mason's daughters. How do you think we keep up with all the gossip? We talk to each other. Unlike some nomad lions I could mention." Lily turned and left the room.

"Grandma, what is she talking about?"

"Years ago Dr. Mason found a shifter who had been injured. He helped him and didn't call the authorities to report what he'd found," Lena replied. "He kept our secret and protected the community. With all the shifters who live here in Hermosa and Bristol Hills, it would've been disastrous for us all."

Obviously proof of shifter activity would've brought all kinds of scrutiny, including from people who would've been happy to go shifter hunting.

"After that, the doctor set up his practice to help the shifters and he got some other doctors to help too," Lena continued. "He's still a very good friend to us."

"So that's why you gossip about him and his family?"

"Mac, we stay safe by keeping in touch with each other. It's not gossip. Not really." She headed over to get a refill of coffee. "But if she is his daughter, then that explains why she's so accepting of you."

"But I don't understand. She knows I go to Dr. Hill. She would've told me she was her sister."

"Maybe she didn't think to mention it," she said. "Really, Mackenzie, if you were more connected to the rest of us you would've known who she was."

"I'm a nomad, remember?" That's what he got for not gossiping. Everyone knew who Zora was but him.

"Not anymore. You'll be mated soon." Lena grinned and returned to her seat at the counter. "I was a bit worried, Mackenzie, but now I'm not. She's a good choice. Her family will accept you and our people will accept her."

"Grandma, why does that matter?"

"Because, whether you want it or not, you have a certain position. Your father is leader of the pride."

Maybe so, but he still couldn't understand why Zora hadn't told him who she was related to. Unless she didn't know about her dad's connection to the shifter world. It still didn't explain why she hadn't told him she was Diane's sister, though. Whatever the truth was, he was going to find out.

"Speaking of your father, I think you should go see him. The challenge is coming and you can give him your support."

"I'm not challenging him, Grandma," Mac insisted. "I told them that."

"I know. But if you're there, the pride will know there are no bad feelings between you and your father. Please, Mackenzie. Do it for me. Stephen will be hurt if his eldest son isn't there."

Once Lena asked something of him, it was hard to resist. "I can't leave my business right now."

"It's only for a couple of days. You know I don't hold much stock in challenge rituals, but this one is a major one for your father. I know him. He's my son and I know how important it will be for you to go."

Though his grandmother hadn't been surprised when he refused to return to help run the winery, his decision had been the talk of the town.

Funny how shifters weren't that much different from humans when it came down to family expectations. Children were expected to follow what had always been done so they could preserve the traditions.

If Mac could break with tradition and remain nomad, what might happen if their children made similar choices? What was funny was that a lot of younger people were already turning away from the rituals. Or they saw them as quaint diversions.

His success had changed a lot of minds, and most of the community had been genuinely supportive. Yet, he still had to fulfill some obligations rooted in the old ways. This was one of them.

"All right, all right." He didn't want to do it, but he couldn't refuse her. "I'll go, Grandma. But I'll drive out there alone. I need time to think. Chris can get back by himself."

"Fair enough. Just stand with your father while he officially gives up leadership. Once Chris is ready, he'll take over. In the meantime, Stephen can guide and prepare him."

"He's not a kid, when is he going to grow up?" Mac asked.

"He will when it's time, Mackenzie. Just as you did," Lena said. "When you return, I want to meet Zora. No excuses."

"Sure." Suddenly he wasn't so thrilled with bringing them together. Zora hadn't been honest with him, and he needed to know why.

The shifters lived with humans and were hiding in plain sight. But that didn't mean they could completely let down their guard. He needed to trust whoever it was he brought into his life. If she could deceive him so easily, was she really the right person for him?

10 BETRAYED

Though Mac was anxious to speak to Zora, he let his grandmother to talk him into staying for lunch. They sat enjoying sandwiches made from leftover steak, while he filled her in on the new coffee bar. Usually he was too busy to take time to sit and talk. Lena had always been there for him and always would be.

When he finally got to the shop, Zora, Gina and Mike were behind the counter. Lunchtime was always busy, so he went straight to the back and didn't interrupt her. Before he put on his apron, he ducked into the bathroom to wash his hands.

Standing there in front of the mirror, he thought of the conversation he'd had with Zora when he'd revealed what he was. She'd looked surprised, and had taken a few moments to respond. But looking back on it now, it had seemed like she'd been too understanding much too quickly. Instead of questioning it, he'd been pleased.

"Mac, is everything okay?"

When he spun around, Zora was in the doorway. "Yeah, sure. Busy out there, huh?" He punched the hand drier and held his hands under the hot blower. "How much did we take in so far?"

"I can check...is there something wrong?"

"Look, do you have a few minutes?"

"Sure. Gina's on the register. What's wrong?"

"Let's go out back." He motioned to the rear door. "I have to go visit my parents for couple of days."

"Oh. Is it what your brother came here about?" she asked as she followed him outside.

He held the door for her. "Yeah. Just some family business. Zora, I had a talk with my grandmother today...is Dr. Hill your sister?"

Her mouth fell open and she simply stared at him. By her reaction, he had his answer.

"Why didn't you say something?" He leaned against his car. "Did your sister tell you about me?"

"Of course not." She stood in front of him. "I found out by accident. Really. I was afraid to tell you because I thought you'd get mad at me."

"Why would I get mad? That doesn't make sense."

"But it does. I was doing work for her and I saw her files," she said. "I wasn't supposed to know about you or the others. I didn't know how to tell you."

"How did you know about the job here?"

She bit her lip before she answered. "I didn't. I only came here because...I wanted to meet you. It was stupid."

"You came to meet me? To see the shifter? What was it like, going to the zoo?"

"You know that's not true!"

He hadn't meant to put it so coldly, but what else could it have been? Why come to see him and pretend she didn't know? "You lied to me."

"I didn't. I just didn't tell you."

"Same thing, Zora. How can I trust you? All this time and you never mentioned who you were."

"I was going to tell you at dinner tonight."

"I'm leaving in a couple of hours, so I won't be here for dinner." He shoved his hands into his pockets. "We'd better get back inside."

"Wait, how did your grandmother know?"

"Everyone knows your father. I had to get the gossip from my family to find out the truth." The more he thought about it, the worse he felt. He'd wanted her to be in his life permanently. And now, he felt betrayed.

"Mac, I'm sorry. After we met, everything happened so fast. I was afraid to admit it to you. Please believe me."

"We'll talk when I get back." He eased past her. All his impulses were fighting him, trying to pull him back to her. But he couldn't. Not until he had a chance to think it over.

"Don't walk away," she called. "Let's finish this."

"It is finished, Zora. We've got customers." He held the door open for her, refusing to meet her eyes as she walked back inside.

Somehow he'd have to get through the next few hours. Once he had a chance to clear his head, it would be easier to sort it out.

How could he deal with losing her? No, he wasn't going to think about it. Not now. It was all falling apart. And now he had to go attend some stupid ceremony. Why was everything suddenly so screwed up?

11 GOODBYE

After almost five hours of travelling, Mac arrived at his family property just after sundown. Driving along the unpaved private road, he kept an eye out for the turnoff that led to the house. In human form he didn't have the same night vision he enjoyed as a cat, so he had to rely on his headlights to illuminate his surroundings. If he missed it, he'd be stuck having to drive to the vineyard before he could circle back.

Having the house set apart from the winery helped to protect their privacy. As far as their customers and human workers were concerned, they were just another family of vintners.

It had been Mac's grandfather's vineyard, so of course tradition called for him to carry on after his father.

Mac mashed on his brake pedal when he saw an opening in the shrubbery. Another half-mile and he'd be at the house. Then he could eat and get some rest.

But when he turned onto the private road, he found a jeep blocking his path. Slowing to a stop, he tried to make out the figure in the driver's seat. "Hey!" he called. "What's going on?"

"Who is it?" A man wearing a tan uniform climbed out of the truck, shielding his eyes from the glare of the headlights as he approached the car. "Hey, Mac--is that you?"

"Donny? What's going on? Why are you blocking the road?" It was Mac's adopted cousin, Donny, who also happened to be head of security for the property.

Donny was younger than Mac by about five years, and outweighed him by several pounds of solid muscle. Built like a block of granite, he looked more intimating than he actually was. After Donny's father had died, Mac's father had taken him and his mother into the pride and allowed them to take the MacKinnon name. When they'd been kids, Donny had followed him everywhere and he'd been closer to Mac than his own brother.

"Mac! So glad to see you," Donny said, brushing his shoulder-length wavy hair off his face. "I heard you weren't coming."

"Where did you hear that? I came for the challenge ceremony. What's going on?"

"Man, didn't anybody tell you? Eldon Durant and some of his buddies are here. They came into our territory to start shit," Donny replied. "He's forcing your dad to fight him for control of the pride."

"But I thought the challenge ceremony was a formality. Dad's supposed step down and give control to Chris," Mac said. "Challenges can't come from outside the pride. This has to be a mistake." Eldon's father, Matthew was a friend of the family. How could he betray them like this?

Donny shook his head. "I wish it was. If Eldon wins, he'll be able to claim authority over the property and everything on it...including us."

"But they can't do that. We've been on this land for generations. The vineyard is here and so is our home," Mac protested. "No way are they going to--"

His cousin interrupted him with a wave of his large hand. "It's challenge law, Mac. Your father told me all about it. It sounded crazy to me too," Donny admitted. "Eldon's pals have been riding around here all day. I parked out here to be sure none of them tried to get near the house."

Mac pounded his fist on the passenger's seat. Territorial boundaries were to be respected between prides. It was a sign of disrespect to cross them without permission. "Why is Eldon doing this now?"

"Guess he heard that your dad's about to step down. Eldon's a punk. He probably figured it would easier to challenge your father and win," Donny mused. "Matthew's already said he's not handing over control of the Durant pride to Eldon. I'm sure none of their members would follow him even if he did become their leader."

"But why didn't anybody tell me about this? Chris didn't mention it."

"All this blew up yesterday. I told your dad I would fight the challenge in his place, but he said he has to do it."

"He said what? He's going to physically fight Eldon?" Mac wasn't sure he'd heard right. His father, who spent more time at business events indulging in wines and gourmet foods, was suddenly going to shift into a lion and fight someone half his age?

Donny folded his arms across his ample chest. "Yeah. They have to fight until somebody draws blood. Two lions fighting for dominance...probably would be a good idea to have some medics on hand."

More than likely his father would fight with everything he had to protect his pride. But what if Eldon meant to do more than draw blood? Mac's mouth went dry. "I can't let my father do this."

"It's the leader's responsibility, Mac. But now that you're here, that changes things. Maybe Eldon will back down if he thinks you came here to fight him."

Right now he'd give anything to kick Eldon's ass. But he had to talk to his parents and find out what the hell was going on. "I've got to get to the house. Can you move the jeep?"

"Sure, Mac. I've got a security detail over there. I'll call ahead and let them know you're on the way." Donny headed back to his truck.

One thing was already decided, Mac would have to step in and do the challenge. It was on his shoulders to make sure his family and the pride were safe.

Up at the house, six other jeeps like Donny's were parked along the gravel-covered driveway. Security guards sat in their vehicles, watching as Mac parked on the grass in front of the house.

Normally their duties consisted of watching over the property, or guiding visitors looking for the winery. On much rarer occasions they kept the peace when disputes between pride members got heated.

As he strode towards the house, the guards acknowledged him by inclining their heads, showing their deference to him as the eldest son of the pride leader. It didn't matter that Mac had no interest in taking over, his position as a dominant male in the pecking order commanded respect.

Mac opened the light blue front door and stepped into the main foyer. It looked the same as he remembered. A crystal chandelier hung like a pendant above the grey marble floor. In front of him, a winding staircase led to the bedrooms. Next to the stairs, sat a shiny black Baby Grand piano. No one knew how to play the thing. But it had a dramatic look that no doubt impressed a lot of his parents' business friends.

His father's study was off to the right next to the piano. The room was dark, as was the sitting room across from it. Sometimes it was hard to believe he'd grown up in this ornate mansion with his brother and parents.

Back in Bristol Hills, his mountainside home seemed very small compared to this. The other pride members inhabited smaller homes on the property, and at times Mac had wished he'd lived in more modest surroundings.

"Dad? Mom?" he called. "Anybody here?" His voice echoed through the empty space.

"Mac?" His mother was at the top of the stairs. She slowly descended, her eyes never leaving his. "I didn't expect you to come!" Her blonde hair was pulled back in a perfect bun, and her sleeveless, white dress was simple but obviously from the most expensive store in town.

Ellen rushed towards him, her arms outstretched. "Mac, I'm so glad to see you." She gathered him into her embrace and hugged him tight.

"Why didn't Dad call me, Mom? Donny just told me about Eldon's challenge." Mac breathed in his mother's perfume. It was sweet and flowery, just like she always wore.

"Mac, please don't be mad with him," she said. "He feels he has to be the one to stand up to Eldon. He's the leader and he can't show fear." She released him, but kept her hand resting on his shoulder. "Your father is stubborn and thinks he's still twenty instead of sixty. With his bad knees and his gout, he's not in any condition to keep up with these young lions."

"I know he's got to look strong, but this is dangerous. He can't fight Eldon."

"He never expected to have to fight a challenge at all," Ellen said, not hiding her annoyance. "Your father never agreed with the old ways and all the feuds and challenges that tore the older prides apart. He never wanted this."

"Mom, why is Matthew going along with Eldon's challenge? He's Dad's friend," Mac said.

"Matthew has no control over that son of his," Ellen snorted. "Our pride is the largest one in this part of the country. The Durant pride is losing members and it's not worth challenging his father for control of it. This is Eldon's chance to get a bigger prize."

So, Eldon figured it would be easy to win this challenge and claim the MacKinnon pride for his own. But seeing what a punk he was, Mac was surprised he had the nerve. "What about Chris? He's supposed to take over when Dad steps down."

"Your brother's not ready yet, and to be honest, I don't think he wants it any more than you do." Ellen dropped her hand from his shoulder. "We were hoping you might change your mind. That's why we sent Chris to get you."

"Sending Chris wasn't the best idea." Mac patted his grumbling stomach. "Can I get something to eat? Then I want to talk to Dad."

Ellen led the way past the stairs and into the kitchen. With the white cabinets and the overhead lighting, no matter what time of day it was, the room always looked like it was bathed bright sunlight. "When Chris called this morning and said you weren't coming, we didn't expect to see you."

"I was at Grandma's. I didn't talk to him." Mac leaned against the marble-topped island. Why did Chris tell them that? It figured he'd make things worse.

"We've got leftovers from dinner. Your father wasn't too hungry." Ellen went to the stainless steel fridge and opened one of the long double doors. "Go have a seat and I'll heat it up."

"When's the challenge?" Mac asked as he sat at the round dining table.

"Day after tomorrow. Out in the clearing behind the house." Ellen took out a large plate that was covered in plastic wrap. When she set it on the counter, Mac noticed that her hands were shaking. "Mac, I'm afraid for your father."

"Mom, don't worry. I'm telling Dad that I'll stand in for him. I'll get him to see that it's for the best."

"Will you? Oh, Mac, thank you." Ellen sighed, as she removed the wrap and balled it up. "But now I have to worry about your safety."

"No you don't. I can handle Eldon."

Mac took out his phone. He'd call his grandmother and let her know what was up. Then he'd tell Chris to get his ass back here. Whatever happened, their father needed both of them.

And there was someone else he had to call. Zora.

"Mom, there's something I have to tell you. I'm thinking of getting mated." Might as well ease into it and get his mother's reaction.

"Is she from one of the prides?" Ellen asked, as she took a plate out of the cupboard. "What's her name?"

"She's human and her name is Zora."

"Somehow, I'm not surprised." His mother didn't make eye contact with him, instead she busied herself transferring pieces of meat from one plate to the other. "And she knows what you are?"

"Of course. She knows everything. I love her, mom." For the first time, he'd actually said the words out loud. It was a relief to declare it to his mother and to himself. "When this is all over, I'll bring her to meet you and Dad."

"It won't be easy for her. She'll have to adapt to a new way of life."

"Didn't you?" Mac asked.

"Yes, I did, but it took time." Ellen looked up. "When this is over...I mean when things are back to normal you can have your mating here by the waterfall where your great-grandparents mated."

Another ritual? Not if he could avoid it. "We'll see, Mom."

First of all he had to apologize. Then if Zora forgave him, they could start talking about the future. If only he could skip the challenge and go kick Eldon and his bunch off the property.

"Dinner's almost ready. Go wash your hands."

Mac chuckled. "Yes, Mom." There was something reassuring being home, even under the circumstances.

Hopefully it wasn't too late to mend things. Zora was everything. He should never have left her without saying goodbye.

Zora sat curled up on the couch, a box of tissues, an empty glass and half a bottle of wine on the table next to her. On the TV, some reality show idiot was throwing a chair at somebody. Why did she watch this shit?

Mac had been right. She'd gone to see him out of curiosity just like an animal in the zoo. How could he forgive her for that?

Maybe she should eat something. Wine on an empty stomach wasn't the best thing. Sliding off the couch, she almost hit the floor. Was she that messed up already? When she stood up, her head spun and she had to steady herself. That's what she got for drinking her dinner.

The phone rang. It was Mac's ringtone. She'd chosen a sound like an old telephone so she'd be sure to hear it even when her phone was in the bottom of her handbag.

Rushing to the dining table, she almost tripped over her own feet. She grabbed her bag and turned it upside down, dumping out the contents. Most of the objects landed on the table, but her phone dropped on the carpet and bounced.

She dropped to her knees, crawled under a chair and grabbed it. Fumbling with the screen, she swiped a few times before she was able to answer.

"Mac? Mac!" Zora leaned against the chair for support. "Answer me!"

"Babe, I don't have much time. I just wanted you to know that--okay, just a minute!"

"What is it? What's going on?" She heard voices in the background, but couldn't make out what they were saying.

"Zora? Zora, I'm sorry I blew up. I'm sorry!"

"No, I'm sorry. I should've told you."

"I have to go. My Dad's waiting for me," he said. "Look, I have to do something. I might not...I...Zora, I love you. Remember that, no matter what happens."

"Mac! What's going to happen?" She was on her knees, hanging on to the chair as she tried to stand up. "Mac, tell me what's going on!"

More talking in the background. Sounded like two or three voices. Why wasn't he answering her?

"I can't go into it now. I'm sorry, babe. I've got to go. I love you. Goodbye."

"No! Mac, don't hang up!" she shouted, staring at the phone as though she could see his face gazing back at her. "Mac, please tell me what's happening!"

But it was too late. He was gone.

12 LION'S PRIDE

The next morning Zora could barely stay focused on the road as she drove to the shop. Mac hadn't called her back, or answered any of her calls or texts. Nothing. Trying to locate his grandmother hadn't worked either. All she had to go on was the MacKinnon last name, and as she discovered, there were a couple hundred of them living in Hermosa. Unfortunately she didn't know his grandmother's first name, so she had no way of narrowing down the list.

When she pulled into the rear lot of the coffee bar, she was surprised to see a red compact in her regular spot. None of the staff had a car like that. Was someone waiting to get the first cup of coffee? It was barely 6:00 a.m., and they didn't open until 7:00. As she parked next to the car, she was relieved to see Mac's brother sitting in the driver's seat.

By the time she got her key out of the ignition, Chris was standing by her door, a big smile on his face.

"Hey Zora! I'm glad I took a chance to come find you," he said.

"Chris, what's going on?" She jumped out of the car. "Mac called me. What happened?"

"It's a long story. I'm on my way back home now. Do you want to come with me?"

"Of course! Gina should be here in a few minutes. She can take care of things while we're gone."

"Mac didn't want me to bring you, but I thought you'd want to come," he said. "He talked to Grandma last night and told her about the challenge. I couldn't believe it. Everything was fine when I left there."

"What challenge?"

"It's a ritual. Two lion shifters have to fight when one challenges the leadership of the other," Chris replied. "Mac's standing in for our dad." Fighting and challenges? What was this crazy shit? Zora headed for the door, her keys in hand. "Mac didn't tell me anything like this. Who's challenging your father?"

"Some asshole named Eldon Durant. He's a punk and Mac's going to kick his ass," Chris said. "Mac's got this handled."

"But what is this about? Why does he have to fight at all?"

"I promise you, there's nothing to worry about." He followed her inside. "I'll fill you in on the way."

Gina showed up a few minutes later, and Zora quickly gave her instructions. Afterwards, she and Chris went by her place so she could drop off her car and pack a bag.

About an hour later they were on the freeway heading up to Napa Valley. She'd never been there before, and if it wasn't for the circumstances, she'd be looking forward to visiting.

While they rode along, Chris filled her in on the challenge ritual. She could tell he was trying to be nonchalant about it, but his reassurances only increased her dread.

"I don't understand why Mac has to fight," she said. "Who is this Eldon? Why is he doing this?"

"Usually challenges don't come from outside the pride. This took everybody by surprise," Chris replied. "But if Mac doesn't fight, Eldon wins by default. It's challenge law, Zora."

Mac had never mentioned any of this when he'd told her about the prides. "I still don't understand why he challenged your father."

"Eldon's always been jealous of us. His father lost a lot of money investing, and his pride's been losing members," he said. "Our pride's bigger and has more land. This is his way of getting control of it."

How was it possible that a few days ago things had been so normal? Now Mac would be fighting another shifter. What if he was killed?

Just the thought of losing him felt like a punch to the gut. No way would she be able to get through this and stay calm.

"Don't worry, Zora. I told you, Mac's got this," Chris assured her. "By the way, he told Grandma you two are going to be mated. I knew it."

"Wait a minute. What do you mean by mating?"

"Look at this traffic. This drive is going to take forever." Chris pulled his visor down. "I left my sunglasses someplace."

"What do you mean by mating?"

"Doesn't bright sun bother your eyes? Maybe it's a shifter thing."

"Answer me, Chris!" Why was he so exasperating?

"It's a lion shifter marriage ritual sort of thing. I've never been invited to one. But from what I hear, there's a lot of sex involved." He patted her knee. "That sounds like fun. But I guess you guys do that a lot already."

When Mac had asked her to move in, he hadn't mentioned any of this. "Marriage and mating?"

"Sure. Shifter lions get hitched pretty fast once they meet the right person. Me, I'd rather take my time."

Zora slumped in her seat. They'd talked about safe sex, monogamy, and love--but mating had never come up in any discussion. What other surprises were waiting for her?

Chris reached over to the glove box. "I threw a couple of bags of chips in there. Can you take one out for me? You can have the other one if you want."

"I'm not hungry." She grabbed one of the bags, opened it and held it out for him. "Your mom's human. How does she manage being mated to a shifter?"

"Okay, I guess. Mom and Dad get along fine," Chris said as he crunched. "By the way, once Mac wins, he'll be the pride leader. Dad wanted me to do it, but I'm okay with Mac taking over. He's the eldest."

"But Mac said he didn't want it."

"Yeah, I know. He'll probably get Cousin Donny to oversee things. Mac will still have the position, though. It'll be his right." He grabbed another handful of chips. "Fine with me. I'm not ready for all those pride leader rituals and stupid shit."

Zora wasn't sure if she was ready for it either. Mac had always given her the impression that he didn't care about following shifter traditions. "If Mac's the pride leader, what would that make me?"

"Grandma's the female head of the pride. When you become Mac's mate, you'll be the second female in seniority."

"Above your mother?"

"Yeah. Mom won't mind. She and Dad are always busy running the business. Grandma is the senior female because the pride is really hers. Her name is

MacKinnon, and when Dad took over as leader, he took that name for the pride." He shoved the remaining chips into his mouth and shook off the crumbs. "What's that nail polish you're wearing?"

"Huh?" Zora held out her hand. "It's teal." Did Chris ever stick to one topic? "But if it's your grandmother's pride, why is your father the leader?"

"I don't know. Back when she was younger, there was a challenge and my grandfather lost. She had to take over for him and lead the pride. Then when Dad got old enough, he became the leader. You'll have to ask Grandma about the details." He emptied the bag into his mouth and crunched. "What kind of color is teal? It's not blue. It's not green. How do they come up with that shit?"

Sticking with one conversation was next to impossible with him. "Chris, I don't know anything about the pride or what I'm expected to do as Mac's mate," she protested.

"You'll figure it out." He wiped his hand on his jeans. "Wish I'd brought a napkin. Got one in that bag?"

Tissues would have to do. She dug the pack out of her handbag. "Who made up all these challenge laws and rituals?"

"Shifter lions have traditions going back hundreds of years. That's what Grandma told me." Chris took the tissue from her outstretched hand. "Zora, there's no need to worry. Trust me."

Don't worry? It was way too late for her to stop worrying. Sighing, Zora leaned against the headrest and closed her eyes. As exhausted as she was, she was desperate for a nap, but she couldn't relax. This was going to be a very long ride.

Almost five hours later they turned off on Rt. 29, a road that wound through various towns in the valley.

"It won't be much longer," Chris remarked. "MacKinnon is near Howell Mountain."

"MacKinnon? Your town is named after your family?" Zora asked.

"Yeah. It's small, but we have our own zip code, 94554."

"Your family has a whole town and zip code?" Was Chris making this up?

He laughed. "So you believe in lion shifters, but having a town named for my family is unbelievable?"

"Now that you put it that way, forget I said anything." She stared out over the passing scenery dotted with stately oak trees. The mountains beyond were a dark green smudge on the horizon. "Is the winery named after your family too?"

"No, it's called Lion's Pride. We have chardonnay and pinot noir, cabernet..."

"I think I have a lot of learning to do," she admitted. Lion's Pride? Talk about hiding in plain sight.

Sure enough, about a half hour later they came up to a maroon-colored sign proclaiming that they were in the town of MacKinnon. A few feet beyond that, Chris turned off on a smaller road rimmed with towering oaks trees. The road inclined a bit as they went up the hill, and then evened out.

Anticipation made her body tingle with anxiety. She was desperate to see Mac, yet fear gripped her at the same time. But once they were together, she knew it would all right. It had to be.

Chris slowed down and turned onto a dirt road that was even narrower than the one they'd been on.

"What the hell?" he asked, bringing the car to a stop. "Shit. It's Eldon."

Up ahead a jeep blocked the road, and standing next to it were two men. One of them was tall and slim, with stringy blond hair hanging to his shoulders. He was wearing a blue and white striped button-down shirt and washed out jeans. The other one was shorter and dumpier, with dark brown hair pulled into a ponytail. His stomach looked like a bowling ball under his green t-shirt, and his jeans were ripped at the knee.

"Which one is Eldon?"

"He's the tall stupid looking one. The other idiot is his cousin, Larry." Chris turned off the car and opened the door. "Stay here."

He got out and approached the men. They watched him warily, and then nudged each other.

"Hey, Chris. Come to help Mac? He's too cowardly to fight me by himself, huh?" Eldon asked. "Who's in the car?"

"Move your truck and get off our property," Chris snapped.

Larry pointed in her direction. "It's a girl. Chris brought his girlfriend. Isn't that cute," he taunted.

"Get the hell out of here," Chris shoved Larry so hard he stumbled backwards. "She's going to be Mac's mate. If he hears about this, he'll rip you both apart."

"His mate?" Eldon smiled. "Hey, Larry, go check her out. Get her scent."

"Stay away from her!" Chris tried to stop Larry, but Eldon grabbed him from behind.

Larry ran over to the car, his stomach jiggling. "Hey, let me look at you!"

Zora threw herself across the seat and pressed the door locks as Eldon's cousin approached. When he got to the door, he leaned in through the open driver's side window. At least his bulk stopped him from doing more than getting his head in.

"Hi there. What's your name?" He smiled, revealing yellowish teeth.

"Leave me alone!" If he tried to get in, she'd hit him with her handbag. It was heavy enough.

Larry sniffed the air and his smile grew wider. "Human! I love human women." He straightened up and called out to his cousin. "She's not a shifter!"

"Even better. This is perfect. Just perfect," Eldon said. "I'm glad you brought her, Chris. You just did me a big favor." He tightened his grip, keeping an arm around Chris' neck.

"What do you want to do, Eldon?" Larry asked, his ample stomach heaving like he'd run several miles. "I'll bet Mac would pay plenty if we snatched--"

"Shut up you asshole! I told you about talking too much!"

"Fuck you, Eldon!" Chris pulled out of Eldon's clutches, swung and punched him in the face.

"Chris!" Zora gripped the seat next to her, digging her fingers into the soft leather.

Larry rushed into the fray and they all fell back and vanished from Zora's line of sight. All she could hear were groans and cursing. Her heart racing, she knew she had to do something to help.

Grabbing the steering wheel she mashed on the horn, and then opened the door. But before she could stick her leg out, she saw a furry shape emerge from the bushes. Then another and another. Lions. Oh my God. In total, there were three large lions with their teeth bared.

She took deep breaths to calm herself. It's okay. They're shifters. They won't hurt me. It's okay. But how was she supposed to stay calm with three lions right outside the car?

Suddenly a man wearing a tan uniform appeared from behind the jeep. In looks and build, he looked like he could've been The Rock's little brother, only there was nothing little about his bulging muscles. "Get up! Get the hell up!" He dropped down and when he stood up again, he was gripping Eldon and Larry by their arms.

"Donny!" Chris stood and wiped his hands on his t-shirt. It was torn and streaked with dirt.

"What are you two doing here?" Donny shoved them both against the truck. "Get off our property. Come here again, and I'll let the lionesses handle it. Now get back to your camp where you belong."

Lionesses. That explained why they didn't have the fur covering their heads. Not that she was an expert on lions, but at least she knew that much.

"Get off me!" Eldon tried to break free. "Chris attacked me and ripped my damned shirt. Do you know how expensive this fabric is?"

"I won't tell you again." Donny shook him for emphasis. "Get back to your camp now." He let them go and rubbed his hands like he was trying to wipe off something dirty.

"I'll go. But when the challenge is over, this will be my pride and my property." He stared at Zora. "And she'll belong to me too. I'll make Mac watch me take her."

His icy, cold stare pinned her against her seat. She couldn't move or even react to his words.

Chris lunged again, but Donny stood in his way. "Stop it, Chris. Don't let him goad you."

"Let's go." Eldon gestured for Larry to follow him. Trailed by the lionesses, they walked past the car and down the road.

Donny came to her door. "It's okay, you can get out now." He motioned for her to open it.

She complied and stepped out, but her legs were shaking so much she could barely stand. "I'm--I'm Zora."

"Hey, Zora. I'm Mac's cousin, Donny." He slid an arm around her shoulders. "Don't be afraid. You're safe. Come with me. I'll drive you to the house. Chris, follow me in the car."

Donny helped her into the jeep and he jumped into the driver's seat. He threw the vehicle into reverse, then straightened up and headed down the road.

"They must've been watching me. I had to go back to the house for something. I'm going to have the lionesses patrol the road from now on. Eldon's got about 10 of his friends camped outside the boundary of our property. He's supposed to stay out there, but he's coming on our property to taunt us."

Donny was driving fast enough for the wind to blow her hair over her face. Not to mention that he was hitting every bump in the road. She held her hair back with one hand, and braced herself with her other.

"Where's Mac? I need to know what's going on," she shouted so she could be heard over the wind and noise of the truck.

"He's out in the woods with his father, getting himself ready. Look, I'm sorry about what happened. Eldon smelled your fear, that's why he acted up. He likes to bully people," Donny replied. "Chris shouldn't have let you come. This is too dangerous."

"I had to be with Mac." She clutched the door as they hit a hole and she bounced on the seat.

"Mac's going to be pissed. It's the challenge laws, Zora. Eldon's full of shit, but what he said is true. If Mac loses..." Donny pulled up in front of the house. "Here's the house. I'll let him explain it."

It was more than a house. It was a mansion with a flagstone front walk and an oversized, light blue front door. Inside, it was just as ornate with a dramatically curved staircase and grand piano in the entryway. It looked like something out of a movie set.

"Aunt Ellen!" Donny called out.

A woman wearing cream-colored slacks and a dark, sleeveless blouse stepped out into the foyer. Her blond hair was pulled back, revealing a perfectly sculpted face. She looked like a she could've been an actress or a model.

"Are you Zora? Mac showed me your picture." She held out her hand. "You're very lovely."

She didn't feel lovely right now. Her hair had been blown all over the place, and she was tired and still shaking from their encounter with Eldon.

"Thank you." She shook Ellen's hand. It was obvious that Chris resembled his mother with his pale coloring and blonde hair, though her hazel eyes were the same color as Mac's.

"My son is out in the hills with his father. He has to get himself ready for the challenge."

"Aunt Ellen, Eldon and his cousin snuck back on the property. They know she's here." Donny rested his hands on his trim hips. "Chris is parking the car. He got into a fight with them."

"What?" Ellen clasped her hands, and then nervously rubbed them. "Make sure Eldon and his group stay on the other side of the boundary. Zora, come with me."

"I'll get your things out of the car and bring them up," Donny said, as he walked back outside.

"Ellen, when is Mac coming back? Is he all right?" She trailed Ellen up the stairs.

"He's fine." She led the way down a short corridor, opened a door and turned on the light. "This is Mac's old room. We turned it into a guest room, but he stays here when he visits."

It was large with dark blue walls, a king-sized bed in the middle, and a seating area at the other end.

"The bathroom is over there." She pointed to a door across the room. "Are you hungry? I'll have something brought up."

"Ellen, please tell me what's going on. Why does Mac have to do this?"

"It's part of our laws, Zora. I know they might sound strange to you, but we still obey them. My son decided to stand in for his father and I'm very proud of him," she said. "Mac told Chris not to bring you here. He's been very irresponsible."

"I couldn't let Mac face this alone."

"According to the law, if Mac is..." She shuddered and lowered her gaze. "If my son loses the fight, Eldon will have the right to take over the pride and our land. You'll be in danger."

"Why? What are you saying?"

"In the old days, back when Mac's grandmother was a young woman, a victor had the right to claim the mate of the defeated lion shifter."

"Claim? You mean make me go with him?" What was this? Some medieval shit? "I'm not a shifter, Ellen and I'm not a prize to be claimed."

"I know that, Zora. But he could demand it, and if Mac is...if he can't..." Ellen rubbed her forehead. "I'm afraid what will happen if he loses. The pride might follow Eldon because they think he'll be a stronger leader. When my son left here to go to college, he never returned. They need to know he hasn't rejected them or his heritage. If the pride believes in him, they'll support him. They'll fight Eldon's group, even if Mac loses."

"Is it possible that Mac could lose?" After hearing Chris' assurances, this was the first time she had a reason to doubt.

Ellen sighed. "Yes, it is possible. I don't trust Eldon. My son is stronger, but the strongest lion doesn't always win."

"We have to do something," Zora insisted. "Can't the pride make Eldon leave?"

"Not according to the law. But there is something you can do. Something that will prove to the pride that Mac hasn't rejected them." Ellen grasped Zora's hands. "That way, if Eldon wins, the pride won't follow him."

"What do you want me to do?" Zora asked, her voice shaking.

"Mac told me he loves you and he's chosen you to be his mate. I want you to perform the mating ritual here before the challenge. Everyone's been on edge since this started. You can give them something to fight for."

A shiver went through her as she realized what Ellen was asking. She tried to swallow, but her mouth was dry. Unable to look away from Ellen's gaze, she fumbled for the right words to reply. "If we do it, the pride will support him?"

"Yes," she replied. "When my son claims you in front of them, you will become one of the pride, Zora.

You'll be a MacKinnon. And if they have to fight...they'll protect you until their last drop of blood."

13 TRUST ME

A few hours later Mac padded into the house through the rear entrance. A large cut-out in the back door allowed him to slip through while still in lion form. With the security patrols protecting the house, at least he could relax now.

All the time he'd been running the hills with his father, he'd been ill at ease. Expecting a confrontation at any minute, he'd overreacted when he'd done some warm-ups for his fight. He'd left himself open a few times, and his father had been quick to cuff him to show him his mistakes. His father wasn't in shape enough for a challenge, but he hadn't forgotten how to handle himself.

On the way back, the lioness hunters had watched out for intruders, and they'd managed to scare off a few of Eldon's pals who'd tried to test them. Obviously, Eldon had brought several hangers-on who were expecting to claim a few spoils. But as rag-tag as they were, Mac knew better than to underestimate them. They had more experience in shifter form than he did.

He headed up the back stairs and continued to his bedroom door. Sniffing the air he caught his mother's scent--and another one. If he didn't know better...

Mac crouched over and willed himself back into human form. As he felt the movement of bone and sinew, the familiar ache radiated out from his groin as his body transformed from animal to human.

Changing from lion form always stimulated and aroused him, making him desperate for physical release. Maybe it was the act of transformation, or a flood of hormones, or his body's fight to retain the animal within the man. He had no idea. When he'd asked Dr. Hill to explain it, she'd come up with all kinds of clinical explanations that had almost put him to sleep.

Maybe he should start calling her Diane seeing how, if he survived the challenge in one piece, he'd be her brother-in-law.

But if he didn't make it out in one piece, he'd have to let Zora go. No way would he keep her tied to someone who was maimed, or maybe worse. He didn't want to think that way, but he couldn't help it.

Mac stood up and shivered as the cool air hit his sweat-covered skin. He opened the door and froze. Zora was lying on his bed. She was wearing her work clothes, khaki pants and denim shirt. Her shoes were by the bed where she'd kicked them off. Her feet were bare and he could make out bright blue polish on her toes.

What was she doing here? Chris. He'd contacted Zora even after Mac had told him not to go to the shop. Mac closed the door and stood watching her as she slept. As glad as he was to see her, he wished she hadn't come.

She stretched and her eyes popped open. "Mac!" She rolled off the bed and launched herself into his arms.

"Zora! You shouldn't have come here!" He held her and lost himself in a kiss.

She broke the kiss and gazed up at him. "Mac, I tried to call you back. Why didn't you answer? I left you messages. I texted."

"Babe, I couldn't do it." Hearing her voice again would've been too much, and he'd needed to stay focused. But now that she was here, it was different. "I was angry before and I shouldn't have been. I'm sorry."

"I should've told you. But Diane was so mad at me. I though you would be, too."

"Don't worry about it. It's okay now." He lifted her off her feet and lowered her onto the bed. "We're together now."

"Mac, your mother said if you---if something happens to you Eldon would have a right to me," Zora said, her voice trembling.

"Babe, nothing will happen to you. I swear it. I won't let it happen. No one will hurt you." All he wanted now was to touch her and feel her against him.

Straddling her, he tugged at her top, pulling it open and sending buttons flying across the room. He kissed her as he eased her out of her shirt, then flung it aside.

"Mac, I want to be your mate and part of your pride," she said. "I want to be with you."

A rush of heat seared him, escalating his hunger to join with her. She was his love, his chosen mate. No matter what happened with the challenge, she'd be there for him. Accepting him. Loving him.

His chest heaving, he braced himself on his forearms and took a few calming breaths before he continued. The animal inside him urged him on, firing his desire to undress her as fast as possible. Even if it meant tearing the clothes off her. He'd been here before, fearful of overpowering her. Afraid she'd turn away in disgust. He didn't want his body to betray him again.

"Mac," Zora whispered, as she stroked his cheek. "It's all right. Don't hold back. We're together now and that's all that matters."

Her lovely brown eyes were full of desire, and there was no fear there. No revulsion either. It was okay. She slid her arms around his neck and eased her tongue into his mouth.

This time he broke the kiss. It was good and he liked nothing better than tasting her that way, but he couldn't hold back any longer. Mac reached under her bra and squeezed her breasts. She closed her eyes, a moan escaping her lips as he fondled her.

His own ache brought him to the point of exploding, as he gently pushed her back against the pillows. Scampering down, he unsnapped her pants and yanked the zipper down. Pulling them off was easy enough, and a moment later they were on the floor next to her shirt.

Zora opened her legs, waiting of him to remove her underwear. He would, but he wanted her to do something first.

"Turn over," he said.

Immediately he sensed her anxiety at his request. Usually he preferred to maintain eye contact with her so he could watch her reactions. But the craving that gnawed at him drove him to possess her, and to fully give himself to her in the most natural way. The shifter way.

"Please, babe. I won't hurt you."

"I know that, Mac. That's why I'm here." She complied and settled herself on her stomach.

Anxious to free her of her remaining garments, he pulled the bra hooks until they gave. In between kisses applied to her back and neck, he eased it off her and sent it to join her other clothing. Only one item left. Taking his time, he smoothed her lacy panties over her rounded hips and down her legs. His senses heightened, the scent of her arousal made his mouth water.

Leaning back on his knees, he grasped her waist and positioned her so that she was on her knees, her butt sticking up. He reached between her legs and slid two fingers between her folds. She was so wet already, and he wanted her wetter. Stimulating her, he alternated between squeezing her clit and easing his fingers in and out.

"Mac, please," she moaned. "You're driving me crazy!"

Normally he'd let things build a bit longer, draw it out to continue to pleasure her. But he was on the brink of exploding, and it was time.

Sliding one hand up to grasp her waist, he eased into her. At first he felt resistance as she clenched, and then she relaxed and he continued to fill her. She was on all fours now, her breasts hanging. Sliding his hand under her for support, he thrust all the way into her.

She cried out and trembled. It felt so good to be inside her warmth. Grunting, he positioned his hands so that he had a firm grip. Unable to restrain himself any longer, he pulled back, and then thrust again, and again. She whimpered as he continued, each time going deeper. Zora pressed her body against him as he pumped, their bodies slapping together.

"That's it, baby. Yes...yes..." he groaned.

With each slap of their bodies together he felt her need answering his. She cried out. Raw and unafraid,

Zora's responses drove him, fueled him, and pushed him to the edge.

She shuddered and trembled. Her arms wobbled as she fell down to the bed, her orgasm echoing through her body. With his grasp still secure on her, he continued to thrust until he felt his own release coming. Gripping her as he moaned her name, he shuddered and collapsed on top of her.

Giving himself a moment for awareness to return, he rolled onto his back, keeping an arm across her. Zora's face was buried in the pillow and hidden from him.

"Babe, are you okay?" He always had to reassure himself that she was all right.

She didn't respond at first. But a moment later, he heard her muffled reply. "Yes, I'm okay."

Exhausted, he closed his eyes and waited for the thundering in his chest to slow. Finally he turned on his side and pulled her so that she was spooned against him. Her skin was slick with sweat and heat.

"How about you? Are you okay?" she asked.

"Without a doubt."

"Mac, you never told me what was bothering you the other night at my place."

Pictures flashed in his mind of that evening when he'd been unable to make love to her. The shame of it was still hard to talk about. "I'm fine now. It was nothing."

"No, it was something, Mac. Tell me," she insisted.

Sighing, he wasn't sure what to say at first. But he knew she wanted the truth. "I was afraid if I didn't hold back, I'd hurt you. Then you wouldn't want to be with me," he blurted.

"Your mom's human, and she manages, doesn't she?"

Not that again. "I know, babe. But I wasn't thinking clearly. Besides, I usually don't think about my parents like that."

"Didn't you tell me shifters weren't shy about sex?"

"They're not. But the human part of me doesn't want to think about my folks doing the deed." He threw his leg over hers. "So let's change the subject. Please."

It was quiet for a few moments, and he felt himself drifting off. Too bad they couldn't just stay here and enjoy each other, and not have the challenge looming over them.

"Is it true that if you lost the challenge, Eldon could claim me?" she asked.

Yet another topic that he was desperate to avoid. If only Chris had listened to him, Zora would be safe at home.

"That will never happen. As long as I have breath in my body you'll never be harmed by anyone. They'll have to kill me first," he replied.

"Don't say that!"

"Shhh." He nuzzled her. "A lioness is a partner. She hunts and stands with her mate to meet all danger. We'll get through this together."

"I'm not a lioness."

"You're as brave as one. So don't worry. I need you to be strong for me. Okay?"

"Mac, I want us to get mated before the challenge."

"No, babe. You've been through enough. I'm not putting you through some ritual just to please--"

"Your pride is here, Mac. Let them see that you want to lead them," she said.

"They'll see it when I fight. It's bad enough you're in the middle of this shit." This was all his fault. By bringing her into this world and wanting her to be his mate, he had put her in danger.

He never considered that anybody would dig up these old traditions. Challenge laws and mating rituals. How the hell had he gotten pulled into this?

If he'd controlled himself and denied his attraction to Zora, she wouldn't be in this position now. But he hadn't been able to help it, and now he was responsible for her life as well as his own.

"It's not just about you, Mac." Zora reached up and caressed his face. "I'm in this too."

"I know that, but I know what's best in this case. Trust me."

How could he fight and not have Zora as a distraction? Somehow he'd have to get focused. The future of the MacKinnon pride was in his hands and now so was

Zora's safety. It was up to him to fight Eldon with everything he had.

14 FAMILY MEETING

Mac waited until Zora was asleep, and then he eased out of bed and padded to the bathroom. Leaning over the sink, he splashed cold water on his face. What was he going to do?

No doubt his instincts would kick in and he'd be able to handle himself. But there was the possibility he wouldn't walk away from it. What then? What would happen to his family? To Zora?

He slammed his fists on the wall, narrowly missing the oval-shaped mirror. It was his fault she was in danger. All he'd wanted was to run his coffee bars and have a regular life. But, he wasn't going to let his family down. They were depending on him, and losing the challenge wasn't an option.

When he went back into the bedroom, he got a pair of jeans and put them on. As he zipped them, he glanced at Zora again. He wanted to stay a little longer, but he knew that was impossible. The more time he spent with her, the harder it would be to stay focused on what he had to do.

Mac opened the door, but didn't go out right away. Instead, he stopped to look at her one last time, and then left the room.

As he headed downstairs, he heard voices. When he walked into the kitchen, he found his mother, Chris, Donny, and another woman he didn't recognize sitting at the table having coffee.

"Mac! I'm sorry!" Chris jumped out of his chair and backed up into the island. "I didn't know what would happen."

"Calm down, Chris." Mac waved him off and sat next to his mother. "It's okay."

"Is it?" His brother's expression changed from fear to surprise, as though he hadn't heard correctly. "You're not mad I brought Zora here?"

"I'm mad that Eldon and his pride forced this challenge," Mac replied.

"The Durant pride doesn't want this challenge," his mother corrected, as she set one of the cups in front of him. "And neither does Matthew. It's Eldon and his followers who are behind this."

"Mac, you've been so busy I didn't get to introduce Cynthia. She's my mate." Donny stood up and motioned for the woman next to him to stand. "She and the lionesses have been on patrol."

"Of course," Mac acknowledged. "I saw some of them when I was out with Dad."

Cynthia inclined her head, showing deference. "Glad to meet you. Donny talks about you all the time." She smiled.

From all appearances, Cynthia was certainly the right mate for his adopted cousin. Though her muscular build wasn't as pronounced as Donny's, she was obviously no stranger to lifting weights. Her appearance was deceptively soft, with her short wavy hair and her dark brown, doe-like eyes, but Mac knew she shouldn't be underestimated.

"Mac, do you think Zora wants dinner? It's being prepared on the grill," Ellen said.

Sniffing the air, Mac picked up the aroma of cooked meats. Funny his mother acted so casual as though someone were just flipping burgers. The full outdoor kitchen behind the house was usually manned by a staff of shifter chefs who not only cooked for the pride, but for social events when his parents entertained for the winery.

"She's resting."

"I'll bet. We heard you two from down here," Chris joked.

"What did you say?" Mac lunged across the table, and narrowly missed knocking the carafe over.

"Hey!" Chris almost fell out of his chair trying to duck out of the way.

"Stop it both of you! This is not the time to fight each other. Mackenzie, sit down!" Ellen snapped, bringing the flat of her palm down on the table. "Chris, Zora is going to be your brother's mate. Show respect."

Chris ran his fingers through his tousled hair, but there was nothing he could do about the flush of red that had spread up his neck and across his face. "Yes, mom." He inclined his head towards Mac. "Sorry."

Leave it to Chris to push things too far. For most male lion shifters, jokes like that could lead to someone getting hurt. At the very least, disrespecting a mate could get you a fist in the face.

Mac resumed his seat, but avoided his mother's glare. It wasn't often that she raised her voice, but when she did, it was time to be quiet.

A minute later Donny cleared his throat to break the awkward silence in the room. "We should take Zora over to the cottage during the challenge. We can have the lionesses protect her," he said, glancing at Cynthia.

"The cottage?" Ellen tapped her fingers on her cup. "That's near the road. Are you sure it's safe enough?"

"The gardening cottage? Wouldn't it be better to protect her here?" Mac asked.

The cottage was two rooms filled with garden tools and a rusty old ride-on lawn mower. He and Chris used to take it out for joyrides until their father caught them. They had a landscaping service now, and no need to use the cottage or what it contained. A leftover from his great-grandfather's time, it was only kept up because his mother though it was cute.

"Eldon and his bunch would expect her to be here." Donny sipped his coffee. "Better to have her out of the way."

"I thought she'd want to be at the challenge," Chris remarked.

"No. I don't want her there." Mac grabbed the carafe and almost spilled the coffee when he tried to pour it. "I want you and Donny to guard her tomorrow."

He'd never shifted in front of her, and he certainly wasn't going to have her watch him fight another lion. It would only upset her, and he wasn't going to make things worse.

"We have to stand with you at the challenge," Chris said.

"No. Dad and Mom will be with me. I have to have people I can trust just in case something happens." He cradled the cup between his hands. Maybe he was wrong to prepare for the worse, but it was a possibility. Challenge law might be archaic, but lots of shifters still followed it. Eldon had never been that bright, but somehow he'd learned enough to use it for his purposes.

"Y-y-you mean you'd trust me to protect Zora?" Chris stammered. He grabbed the sugar bowl and emptied half of the contents into his cup.

"Yes, I trust you. You're my brother." Pesky little brother or not, he was a MacKinnon and that bond could never be broken.

Chris grinned. "You'll kick his ass, brother. I'm sure of it."

"Knowing Eldon, I'll bet he's not happy to be challenging Mac. He expected to be fighting Uncle Stephen," Donny said. "He'll fold as soon as he realizes he can't win. The challenge ends when one of your draws blood. Eldon won't have a chance."

"Eldon is sneaky and who knows what he's got planned. If I know Zora's safe, I can keep my mind on the fight," Mac said. "Besides, what if Eldon wins and the pride decides to follow him? They won't stop him from taking her."

"Zora is stronger than you think." Ellen patted his hand. "The pride members are eager to stand with you, if you'll let them. That's why I think she should perform the pre-mating ritual."

"The what?" Mac's head snapped in her direction.

"At the waterfall out by the vineyard. The same place your great-grandmother and father were mated."

"Mom..." Sighing, Mac rubbed his forehead. The dull ache was getting worse by the minute. "What's this about?"

"She has to go to the waterfall and bathe in it. She can do it at twilight. According to the challenge laws, Eldon can't cross the boundary to our property after sundown," she replied.

"If he does, all bets are off and we can go kick his ass off the property." Donny gestured for Chris to pass him the sugar.

"We'll protect her," Cynthia offered. "I'll have some of the lionesses leave their patrol. If his group can't cross over anyway, that's the best time to do it."

"If Eldon wins, he has the right to claim her as his mate. I don't want to expose her to any more danger," Mac snapped.

"Didn't that almost happen to grandma when grandpa lost his challenge? She showed them!" Chris slapped his hands on the table for emphasis.

When the victorious lion had tried to attack Lena, she'd fought him off. By the time her sisters and other members of the pride had joined in, it became a battle that had passed into legend.

But his grandmother was a shifter lion, and had been able to defend herself. Zora didn't have that ability. A human would be easy prey.

"Mac, I promise we'll protect Zora. The pride members are anxious about this fight. If she does this, I'm sure it'll put everyone at ease," Cynthia said.

Obviously this was a bigger deal than he thought. "Okay!" He held up his hands to silence them. "But it has to be her choice."

"Cynthia and I will talk to her," Ellen acknowledged. "You should go on now. Your father is resting.
He'll join you later and spend the night with you out
by the clearing."

Mac pushed back his chair and stood up. The others
followed suit, their eyes on him. More and more it felt
like he had no control over anything going on around
him. Now he had to go prepare for a fight to protect
the pride and the woman he loved.

15 THE BATHING RITUAL

Zora was sitting cross-legged on the bed looking through her overnight bag when she heard a knock at the door. Thinking it was Mac, she didn't look up until she heard Ellen's voice.

"Zora, I'd like to talk to you for a few moments." Hands clasped in front of her, she took tentative steps, followed by a woman wearing a tan uniform.

"Oh, hi, Ellen." She pushed the bag aside and smoothed her shirt down so she looked a bit more presentable. Thanks to Mac her work shirt no longer had buttons. It had been easier to grab one of his and put it on. "Where's Mac?"

"He's getting ready for the challenge." Ellen perched on the edge of one of the chairs across from the bed. "This is Donny's mate, Cynthia." She motioned to the woman who had remained standing at attention by the door.

Cynthia inclined her head in acknowledgement, but didn't say anything.

"Mac doesn't want to do the mating ritual," Zora said. "Do you have any other ideas?"

"He gave me the same response," she admitted. "But there is something else. When shifter lions decide to mate, there are three rituals involved. The mating itself, the introduction to the pride and the bathing ritual."

"Bathing?" After trying to wrap her mind around a mating ritual, now there was something else to think about.

"Yes, before mating, the female performs a ritual to bathe and prepare herself. It takes place at the waterfall on our property."

"Will Mac be there too?"

"No, usually the male doesn't attend." Ellen fidgeted, like she couldn't find a comfortable position in the chair. "But there will be witnesses..."

"Watching me bathe? Seriously?" Zora swung her legs off the bed and jumped up. "People will be watching me? Naked?"

"Yes, just like the mating. Only invited guests, of course, but it's--"

"Wait a minute. Mac and I would be having sex in front of witnesses?" The wind knocked out of her, Zora dropped back down on the bed. Funny how Chris hadn't mentioned that the guests would be watching them. What the hell was this?

"Zora, for shifter lions, nudity is not something to be ashamed of. Neither is sex. It's not voyeuristic. It's like attending a wedding ceremony. They want to share in the joining."

"By watching us have sex and seeing me bathe?" As much as she wanted to help Mac this was more than she bargained for.

Cynthia cleared her throat. "You should know, the waterfall is near the boundary of the property. Eldon and his crew have been camping there. They'll be able to see you."

"What? But, suppose he tries something? You said he'd have the right to claim me," Zora stammered.

"It'll be at twilight and according to the law they can't come on our property without voiding the challenge," Ellen replied. "You'll be safe."

"But they'll see me," Zora said. "You're saying they'll just watch and not do anything?" Twisting the ends of Mac's shirt between her fingers, she fought to keep her composure.

"If they do, the challenge is over. It's not worth it to Eldon to make a move and ruin his chances," Cynthia said. "Besides, some of the other members of the pride will be there, so you'll have friendly people around you."

"How many others?" Zora asked.

"We've asked that each family send one person. It might end up being around thirty or so," she said.

"Watching me bathe under a waterfall. Naked." The way both women were staring at her, she felt like a specimen being studied under a microscope.

"Cynthia, could you leave us? Wait for me by the stairs," Ellen requested.

Mac's mother waited until they were alone before she came over and sat next to Zora.

"Years ago, I was a fashion model. Not a supermodel or anything, but I got regular work for magazines and runways." Ellen slid her arm around Zora's shoulders. "I came here for a photo shoot at Lion's Pride. That's how I met Stephen. He was handsome with dark hair like Mac's. We hit it off right away."

Since Mac's father had been in lion form when she'd arrived, she hadn't had the chance to be formally introduced yet. But she could imagine how Ellen would've felt meeting him for the first time. "When did he tell you he was a shifter?"

"Not until about three months later. I was living in San Francisco, but I travelled all over the world. He'd come to see me, or I'd come here. I realized something was different about him, especially when it came to...when we were together." Ellen's glanced at her. "I think you understand what I mean."

Knowing she was hinting at intimacy with Mac's father should've been incredibly awkward, but it wasn't. "Yes, I do."

"I was away in Paris, then Milan for a couple of weeks. When I returned, Stephen invited me here to talk to me. I knew he was going to propose. But I didn't realize what he was going to tell me afterwards."

"That's when he told you? Why did he wait?"

"He said later that he was afraid if he'd revealed himself earlier in our relationship, I would've broken it off. When he tried to explain, I thought he was joking. So he showed me." Ellen chuckled. "I think I was too afraid to run or even to scream. Then he shifted back to human. I was stunned."

Zora had never seen Mac shift. Whenever she'd asked about it, he'd refused to go into details. "But you didn't run away."

"I was madly in love with him by that point. But I'll admit it took me a little while to accept it, though," she said. "We had our mating by the waterfall. And at the introduction, Lena was there to present us to the pride. She gave us her blessing. Once she did, no one objected to Stephen taking a human mate."

"But why would they?'

"They wanted to be sure the MacKinnon pride would continue and that Stephen wouldn't abandon them for the human world. So many prides have broken apart because of that." Ellen squeezed Zora's shoulder. "That's why I asked you about the ritual.

Mac is the eldest and he should be the one to take over. But if the pride thinks he doesn't care about tradition, they'll think he doesn't care about them either."

"But he does care, Ellen. That's why he's fighting."

"I know that. But they need to see that when you two mate, you'll continue the MacKinnon pride. If Mac loses and the members feel it's not worth fighting for, they'll give up and let Eldon take over. The Durant pride isn't backing him now, but they will if he beats Mac." Ellen squeezed her shoulder again, and then stood up. "There have been so many blood feuds and fights between shifter groups, not just the lions. Since I've been Stephen's mate, we've avoided all that. Until now."

Looking up at Mac's mother, Zora could see the fear and desperation in her eyes. How could she let Mac down when he needed her? If she could do this, it would encourage the pride to rally around him no matter what happened. It was time to move forward into her new life as his mate. "I'll do it, Ellen. I'll bathe at the waterfall."

"Thank you, dear. Thank you." Ellen gathered her into an embrace. "It will be all right. I promise you." She straightened and pushed a stray lock of hair off her face. "I'll get you something to wear."

Not only was Ellen taller, but she was much slimmer than Zora, with straight hips and a much smaller bust. What could she have that they both could wear? "I brought clothes with me," Zora said.

"You'll need a robe. It'll be easier to remove," she replied. "In the meantime, I'll have dinner sent up for you." Ellen's steps were much brisker as she left the room and closed the door behind her.

There was no going back now. But exactly what had she committed herself to? Shivering, she yanked the blanket over her, even though she knew the temperature had nothing to do with it. How was she going to keep it together enough to represent herself as Mac's future mate? If only she could talk to him about it. It might make her feel a hell of a lot better.

A half hour later Mac was throwing the remains of his dinner into one of the large trash bins by the patio. Donny had called most of his security people here to help keep things locked down. Half of them were milling around the outdoor kitchen, keeping the chefs busy.

Shifting took a lot of energy and burned calories faster than any normal human exercise could. Animal instincts could be tough enough to manage when human thoughts were battling for control. A hungry shifter wouldn't stop to think rationally about what he or she was supposed to be doing. They'd just do what came naturally--go after prey. So it was essential to only have one focus once they shifted, and that was to protect the property.

The rest of Donny's security team was on duty making sure no one else entered the private road leading to the house. And still others were over by the winery, ensuring that none of Eldon's friends would end up over there accidently on-purpose.

Mac shoved his hands into his pockets, willing himself to stay calm. If he expended energy now, he'd have less for tomorrow. Even getting pissed off could distract him. Which meant he was working harder than ever to keep Zora out of his thoughts. He could not afford to let human feelings stop him from fighting with all his might.

"Mac!" Cynthia rushed over to him. "Your mother talked to Zora. She said yes to the bathing ritual."

Startled, Mac didn't answer right away. He hadn't expected her to agree without taking time to think. "Did mom persuade her? You know what I mean."

Cynthia lowered her eyes and nodded. "I left the room and they talked by themselves. I'm sure Ellen made it clear what was at stake."

A diplomatic answer if there was one. "Okay. I'm going to be there too. She's not doing this alone."

"Mac, you're supposed to be at the clearing with the others. You have to shift so you can be ready for tomorrow."

"It's only a couple of hours more until dusk. I'll shift after Zora's done."

"What's going on?" Donny walked up, a half-eaten burger in his hand.

"Mac's going to the waterfall," Cynthia said.

Donny shook his head while he tore off a chunk of meat. "You have to prepare. The longer you stay in human form, the longer it will take to get back to being a lion. It's not just your body, Mac, it's your head, too. Your heart--everything in you has to be lined up."

Mac held up his hands as if to hold them both off. "I know that, but I can't let her do this alone."

"We'll be there," Cynthia interjected. "Other members of the pride will be there too."

"She doesn't know them. She knows me. I'll be her mate I should be there." He was tired of having to defend himself. "You're acting like she should be okay with this. She's human, remember?"

"Maybe you're underestimating her," Cynthia said. "She knew you were a shifter and she still decided to be with you. She can't be that scared."

"Look, if this ritual is so important, then I should witness it, too. Right? I'm going." Mac threw his shoulders back and glared at both of them. He knew the body language would enforce his words. Their lion shifter conditioning would kick in and they'd comply.

They both lowered their heads, giving him respect as the dominant male. He hated to pull that one, seeing how he used to hate it when his father pulled it on him. But there was a hierarchy, and it was time he

enforced his position in it, especially if it meant keeping Zora safe.

16 CLAIMED

Two hours later, Zora was riding across the property in an open jeep with Cynthia at the wheel. Thankfully, the evening chill hadn't settled in. Here she was in a light, white satin robe and her flip-flops.

Cynthia slowed down as they pulled up to a clearing. Up ahead was a stream bordered by large rocks.

"This is it." Cynthia parked the jeep and shut it off. "Most everyone's here," she said as she climbed out.

On the right, water poured down from an arrangement of rocks that jutted out from the hill above. It flowed into a small pool that fed the stream.

"Did you have to do this too?" Zora asked as she stepped out, careful to hold her robe to her.

"Yes. Our ceremony was over a couple of days. I was nervous at first. We both were. But it got much better." Cynthia broke into a broad smile.

Sitting on the grass on either side of the stream were about thirty humans and lions. She wondered why some of them shifted and some didn't. But no matter what form they were in, they were all watching her.

Directly in front of her was flat land with no trees, and she could see the yellow glow of a fire about a quarter of a mile away. Most likely Eldon's camp--a direct line from the waterfall. Tall trees formed a canopy over them, shading the area so that only their shapes by the fire were visible.

"Mac's coming," Cynthia said, pointing to her left.

Taking long, easy strides, he walked with assurance, his body unencumbered by clothing, three female lions trotted along behind him.

"I didn't know you were coming!" She tried to run to meet him, but ended up getting tripped up in her flip-flops.

Mac caught her. "I wasn't going to let you do this alone." He gathered her into his arms. "Let's get this done," he said, as he guided her towards the waterfall.

Two short plants sat next to the falls, with their long, flat, pointed leaves, they reminded her of over-sized pineapples.

"What are those?" she asked. "They don't look like the other trees."

"They're not. My great-grandmother planted them."

The murmur of conversation from the spectators was a reminder that she and Mac were the center of attention. They stopped just a few steps away from the edge of the stream. Mac unloosed the belt and eased the robe off her shoulders. Then he helped her to step out of her flip-flops and wade into the stream.

As soon as she put a toe in the water, she had to force herself to step all the way in. It was freezing. He supported her with an arm around her waist, and she stepped up into the pool directly under the falls. Bracing her hand on the rock face, she immediately felt like jumping back out again as the icy water hit her.

"Why is this so cold?" she asked, as goosebumps spread up her arms.

"Don't know. Sorry it isn't warmer," Mac replied, as he joined her.

"Are you supposed to be with me?" she asked. "I thought I was the one who had to bathe."

"At this point, I don't think it matters. No one has said anything," he said, looking over his shoulder at the crowd.

She was still trying to ignore all the eyes trained on her. "Mac, I'm really cold. Aren't you?" Why wasn't he shivering like she was?

"My skin is not quite as sensitive to the cold." He cupped his hands to collect the water, and poured it over her. Washing down her back and arms. "Is that helping?" he asked.

"No!" She folded her arms across her chest and leaned against him. At least his warmth had stopped her teeth from chattering. It figured that shifters would have some extra protection from freezing to death. Whoever thought of having a bathing ritual in icy water had to be nuts.

Mac continued to rub her back. "You're purring," he said.

Purring? Now she'd heard everything. "That's not possible. I'm not a cat." She turned so she could look across the way towards Eldon's camp. The fire was still burning.

"It feels like a purr whenever I do this." He ran his hands down to her hips, then back up again.

"We're supposed to be bathing. I think you've got something else on your mind." She was enjoying it, though. And she wasn't cold anymore.

"You're the one who's supposed to be bathing. I came to watch." His voice was a deep rumble against her ear. Around them it grew darker and the moonlight became more pronounced. Even with the sound of the water, she could hear growls and murmurs around them.

Gradually his back rub became a caress as his lips found hers. Lost in the kiss, she didn't even realize she was pressed against the rock face until he broke away. His eyes were gentle, yet there something else there. An urgent need to satisfy his desire.

"Zora, I don't want to lose you," he whispered. He nipped her ear, and then trailed his lips down to her neck.

"You won't, Mac. There's nothing Eldon or anyone can do about it." She arched her back, grinding her shoulders against the stone as he ran his teeth along her neck. His erection was pressed against her, and she knew what they had to do.

She braced her hands on his shoulders and stood on her toes. "Let's do it now. Let Eldon see us together," she whispered in his ear.

"I'm sure he's already watching. You mean...no babe, I can't. If they run over here, hell's going to break loose. I'm not going to be in any shape to stop them."

"Everyone here will stop them."

"I can't stay aware of him and you. Do you get it? I'll leave myself open."

"Mac, the pride won't let him get to us." She ran her hands down his chest. "Your great-grandparents mated here. So did your parents. So will we." Zora circled his nipple with her fingertip, following it with her tongue. She wasn't a prude, but she'd never had sex in front of an audience before. Maybe it was impulsive of her, but so what. She wanted to claim Mac just as much as she wanted to be claimed. Let everyone witness it and have no doubts.

He groaned and clutched her hips, digging his fingers into her flesh. A long, deep moan escaped his lips and he hoisted her up. In response, she wrapped her legs around him. She gasped as he pressed her against the rock face, getting into position so that he could enter her.

Nestling her head in the crook of his neck, she closed her eyes and lost herself in the sensations of the hard rock rubbing her back and his member easing into her. She moved her hips to allow him easier entry, but she heard him growl against her. Wrapping her arms around his neck, she held on as he continued to sheath himself. She tensed when she heard a roar from across the way, where Eldon's camp was.

"Relax, babe. It's okay. I've got you," Mac said, his voice strained. "I don't want to hurt you. Relax."

No matter how intense things got between them, he'd always been mindful of her. He never wanted anything to go so far that she would be in danger. She had come to realize that the beast inside him wasn't mindless or a monster. If he had been, she'd never have fallen in love with him.

But Mac was capable of driving her to the edge of reason, and that's what she wanted right now. She was a woman who wanted her man, her shifter, to take her and give her what she desired. Humans were animals too, weren't they?

"I know you have me, baby. And I have you. Take me now." She bit his ear lobe, crunching down on it as hard as she could.

He yelped, and responded with a swat on her ass. It stung, but only managed to make her more aroused. Tempted to ask him to do it again, she didn't get the chance. Gripping her, he brought her down hard against him. He repaid her bite by sinking his teeth into her shoulder, all the while moving her in a steady rhythm, up and down.

Pressed against the rock face, her back rubbing against the rough stone, she lost herself in the sensations of intoxicating pleasure radiating from her center. She didn't care about the friction of the hard surface against her skin. She just wanted their connection to continue.

Even the roars and growls didn't frighten her, as the pride members were caught up in the mating fever that burned between them. Water splashed down over them, she turned her head to keep it from getting into her nose and mouth. She could drown under here and she wouldn't care. As long as she felt Mac's hands on her as he possessed her. Taking her in front of his pride, claiming his mate, and defying anyone who would take her away.

Tension built inside her, tuning out everything except Mac's grunts and the sound of her body slapping against his. She knew that he wasn't aware of anything except her. Fire burned between her legs, spreading up into her stomach. Trembling, she sobbed, desperate to release the energy that was building up between them.

In response, Mac's teeth found the same spot where he'd already bitten her. She whimpered, and trembled against him. His movements were more insistent, more determined. Pressing her against the rock face, he held her still and thrust into her, harder and harder.

"Oh my God, Mac!" She cried, aching to come. Then her orgasm hit her, stunning her in its intensity. A white hot haze surrounded her, and she screamed his name over and over.

Roars from Eldon's camp threatened to drown her out, but the pride members answered with roars and calls of their own. Her body jerked and she continued to hold on as another orgasm ripped through her, and another. Spent, her legs began to slide down, but Mac gripped them and lifted her back up. He continued to thrust, then his body tensed.

She leaned back against the stone and let the water wash over her. Squinting to keep water from getting in her eyes, she watched him. His eyes were closed and his mouth open as he gasped, then groaned, then roared. It was so loud that she was frightened that it could be coming from him in human form.

As he leaned his forehead against hers, the pride members responded, by answering his roar, and calling out to him, shouting their approval.

Releasing her, he kept a grip on her waist until she was on her feet again. Swaying, she fell against him and jumped as the frigid water hit her scraped-up back.

They breathed in unison, expelling air like they'd both been running for miles.

Finally, Mac grasped her shoulders and held her so he could look into her eyes. "Come on, let's go." He guided her out of the pool and back onto the grassy bank.

Silvery moonlight washed over them, giving everything a ghostly glow. She saw that the pride members were slowly moving away, heading in the same direction that Mac had come from. Out of the corner of her eye she noticed Cynthia standing by the jeep, the three lionesses sitting next to her.

"Why are they leaving?" Zora asked. "What if Eldon comes now?" Now that it was over, she was feeling anxious again.

"Believe me, he won't come now. I'd tear him to pieces." Mac guided her to sit down on the grass. "Lie on your stomach."

"What are you doing?" she asked.

"Checking your back. Just hold still."

He padded away across the thick grass, then she heard the sound of something tearing and breaking. When he returned, he knelt down next to her.

"What are you--" she began.

"Shhh! Your back is scraped."

Facing him, with her head resting on her arm, she watched him rub his palms together, then she felt his hands gliding along her back.

"This is aloe from the plant my great-grandmother planted. There's a reason she planted it."

It was cool and stopped the stinging. "I didn't know it came in a tree form."

"You need to get outdoors more," he said, continuing to apply the aloe to her skin. "There, that should do it."

"That feels good."

"So should this." He swatted her ass again.

"Hey!" She spun around and ended up sitting on the spot he'd just smacked. "What's that for?"

"That's for biting me."

"You bit me too!" She grabbed his hand and they both stood up. "Twice!"

"I'm a lion. I bite. Remember?" Mac grinned as he picked up her robe.

"And spank too?" she asked. Not that she'd minded it.

"Only when you're bad. Come here." He held the robe open.

After she put it on, he tied the belt. "Now you'd better go to the house. I've got to get back to the clearing. Dad will be looking for me."

"Mac, before you go, do something for me."

"What is it?"

"I want to see you shift."

He backed away, shaking his head. "No, babe. That's not a good idea."

"I'm your mate now. I should know what happens," she said.

"I don't want you to be afraid."

"I'm part of the MacKinnon pride now, aren't I? I love you, Mac. Please don't hide that part of yourself from me."

Resigned, he dropped to the ground and got on all fours. "All right. I'll show you."

Mac closed his eyes and drew in a long, deep breath, expelling it slowly. He repeated that again and again until his body began to transform. A light coat of blondish-brown hair sprouted across his skin. His arms and legs changed shape, expanding and contracting into the contours of a lion's body. A mane of orangey brown hair appeared as the human outline of his face disappeared.

Was she actually seeing this? This wasn't supposed to be possible. It couldn't be. This huge, lion in front of her couldn't be the man she'd just made love with. Legs wobbling, she was caught between running away and being too afraid to move.

Groaning, Mac arched his back in a typical yoga cat stretch as the final adjustments rippled through him, his long tail swiping back and forth. When he turned to her and roared, he exposed his teeth, sharp and menacing.

She took a step back without realizing it, then caught herself and remained in place, keeping eye contact with him. There was no hint of the man who she'd just been with under the waterfall. Nothing human in the gold-colored, cat eyes that examined her.

Swallowing, Zora approached him and got close enough to run her fingers through his thick mane. In spite of her effort to stay calm, she felt adrenaline coursing through her. A voice in her head urged her to run, get away from this powerful beast who could devour her. But instead, she willed herself to stay still as he rubbed his head against her leg. Well, he was a cat, just a really big one.

Shaking his head, he gave her another roar, and then bounded off in the direction he'd come from. As she watched him, she had to catch her breath as her mind reeled from what she'd just seen. Knowing he was a shifter was one thing, but actually seeing it was another. Part of her didn't want to believe it. But it wasn't a special effect in a movie. This was real.

Shaking, she had trouble getting her feet back into her flip-flops. By the time she joined Cynthia at the jeep, she felt her heart rate slowing.

"You've never seen him do that before?" Cynthia asked.

"No. Not until now." She climbed into the jeep. "Are the lionesses coming back with us?"

"Yeah. They'll escort us to the house. But I'm sure we won't have any trouble."

They drove away and headed onto the narrow dirt road that led back to the house. Zora clutched the thin robe around her shivering body. Moonlight bathed their surroundings, though the only other light came from the jeep's headlights.

She wasn't used to being anywhere without any streetlights. Just to be sure they were protected, she glanced over at one of the lionesses who kept pace next to the vehicle. "Mac said Eldon wouldn't dare come across the border after...after we finished. Why not?"

"There are two times when a shifter is dangerous. One is when they're hungry. The animal instincts kick in and they have no choice but to feed. Lions aren't maneaters, but if you're really hungry you'll go after what's available. Not smart if you end up running someplace where a human can shoot you. This isn't exactly the wild."

"And the other time?"

"After sex. Lots of hormones churning. It's hard to be rational while your human and the animal sides are fighting it out. A shifter will lash out if they're at-tacked. Eldon is a punk and a coward. No way would he have come across the boundary after he saw that you two had mated."

"I wasn't exactly planning that," Zora admitted.

"The pride members were very pleased. It gave them hope the traditions will live on and the family will continue."

"But we're not ready to start a family just yet."

"That doesn't matter. The two of you coming to-gether was important for them to see. Especially after

Eldon's foolishness. But now he's an even bigger punk, so that was really sweet," Cynthia said.

"Why do you say that?"

"Mac claiming you in front of Eldon and his gang said that Mac doesn't respect him or his claims. Male lions are big on posturing," Cynthia replied, as she steered around a curve and got on the main road. "It's all about being dominant. Pretty much Mac just gave him a big, fuck you. And so did you."

"Are lionesses like that too?"

"Nope. We have to be more strategic. Lioness hunters can bring down an elephant if they have to. Shifter lionesses are just as tough. We don't have time for all that noise." She slowed down as they approached the courtyard. "Mac's a really good guy. Hard working. So many of these lion shifters just want to lie on the couch scratching themselves while their mates are out there working. Mac's not like that."

"I know. Shit! I forgot to call the shop!"

"Shop?"

"Mac's business. I have to check in and see what's going on," Zora said.

"Now I see why you two make a good pair. Why don't you rest tonight? It'll be a long day tomorrow," Cynthia pulled up in front of the house. "You'll be home soon and you two can get back to normal."

Cynthia was right. Just for tonight she'd let it go. The coffee bar was their real life--or was it? Mac lived in two worlds, and now so did she. "Do I still have to wait at the cottage? Can't I see the challenge?"

"Eldon is a fool, but I can't say the same for his crew. Let's play it safe and keep you protected until it's over, okay?" she asked, as she got out of the jeep. "The lionesses will wait until you go inside. Good night."

"Good night, Cynthia." Her legs were still aching and so were some other parts. But it had been worth it. Mac was hers and she was his, and no one was going to come between them. Just let them try.

17 THE CHALLENGE

The next morning Zora was up at 5:00 a.m. after spending a restless night. All she could think of was the challenge. One of the kitchen staff brought her breakfast, and she tried to force down the omelet and toast.

Donny picked her up at 7:00 to drive her to the cottage. He only had one-word replies when she asked about Mac, and the usually talkative Chris wasn't much better.

Minutes later she was sitting in a rickety chair next to an old riding lawn mower. Both men took turns pacing from one side of the room to the other. From time to time, Chris would stop to look out of the dirt-encrusted window, while his cousin kept his attention on the front door.

"Has it started yet?" she asked. "I don't hear anything."

"You wouldn't hear anything from here. The clearing is a couple of miles away," Chris said. "They'll start around 7:30."

"How does it work? Do they just start fighting?" Unable to keep still, Zora tapped her feet on the dusty floorboards.

"Not right away," Donny replied. "Don't worry, Zora. It'll be okay."

"Why aren't you with him? Suppose Mac needs help?"

"Mac wants us here with you," he said.

"The lionesses protected me yesterday. Why not today? Then you can watch Mac's back."

"This is different, Zora," Chris said. "It's important to Mac that we're here."

She knew they would've preferred to be at the clearing with him. As much as she was glad to have them here, she felt guilty.

"Zora, I heard what happened at the waterfall," Donny said. "I was against Mac going, but I was wrong. It really helped to have the pride witness your mating."

"Yeah. Donny's right," Chris agreed. "Mac's always been so private. They liked that he trusted them."

"Did they think Mac didn't trust them before?" she asked.

"Nothing like that, but he's never been quick to share things. Then when he left, some people thought he was rejecting the pride. You know?" Donny glanced at the door. "I'll be right back. I heard a noise outside."

She jumped to her feet. "Is something wrong?"

"Let me check it out." Donny exited and closed the door behind him.

"Don't be nervous, Zora. I'm sure nothing will happen," Chris said, as he continued to pace in front of her.

A moment later she heard heavy footsteps tramping past the cottage. The door flew open and Donny burst in. "Some of Eldon's people are back by the road. We'd better get out of here!"

Mac woke before sunrise and had gone for a run along the perimeter of the property, Donny and Chris at his heels. When he passed by Eldon's camp, the area was deserted and the remnants of the fire were just smoking ash. Wanting to stay in his animal form, he'd gone deeper into the woods to hunt and feed while his father, Donny and Chris had returned to the house.

Unfortunately, though he'd looked forward to bonding with his father and the others, sleeping under the stars wasn't his thing. Every rustle in the grass had forced him back to alertness. Anxious and eager to get the challenge over with, he'd spent most of the time on edge.

By the time he arrived at the clearing around 7:00, most of the 150 or so members of the pride were already assembled along the sidelines. In keeping with custom, they remained in human form to ensure that no one would interfere with the fight.

Flat and covered with grass, the field was surrounded by sturdy oak trees. Almost two miles away from the winery, it was secluded and perfect spot for two lions to fight.

Mac ran across the field, and then trotted back to the sidelines to wait for the challenge to begin. No need to tire himself out. He'd need all his energy once things got started.

At almost 300 pounds, he'd have to be smart about how he maneuvered. Even though the fight was supposed to stop after drawing first blood, anything could happen once lions got to fighting.

Burning out too early could cost him his life.

Chris grasped Zora's arm and rushed out the door of the gardening cottage. When they got outside he sniffed the air. "Larry's around here someplace. I can smell him."

He's coming and he's not alone. Look!" Donny pointed to a truck heading in their direction, stirring up dust as it trundled down the road. "How did they get through the patrols without being spotted?"

"What do we do now?" Zora asked.

"We can go back to the house. Get your guys off patrol and have them meet us there," Chris suggested.

"Security needs to stay put in case more of Eldon's people come. I have a couple of guys watching the house. That'll have to be enough," Donny said.

Meanwhile the truck was getting closer as Donny and Chris went back and forth. She was tired of hiding from these idiots anyway. "If we have to fight our way out, then we will."

Both men stared at her like she'd sprouted a second head. There was a bunch of gardening tools in the cottage. She couldn't shift, but she could defend herself. Zora ran back inside, grabbed a rusty rake out of the corner and ran back to join them.

"You're going to rake them to death?" Chris asked.

"Let's go. We're wasting time." Donny led them to the jeep.

Zora jumped into the back, while Chris took the passenger seat. Donny gunned the engine and put the jeep in gear. Just as he pulled out, a lion rushed out from the bushes behind the cottage.

"Donny!" Zora yelled, as she swung the rake.

He swerved the jeep so hard that it fishtailed on the gravel. She had to grab hold so she wouldn't fall out.

"Damn it, Donny! Watch what you're doing!" Chris screamed.

"Shut up, Chris!" Donny snarled, as he shifted the gears and mashed down on the gas.

The lion was behind them, and so was the truck. Even though Zora was bouncing around, she could make out Eldon's cousin Larry driving.

"How the hell did they know where we were?" Chris asked.

"Larry got her scent. We should've known he'd track her." Donny turned the wheel to avoid the rocks lining the driveway leading to the house.

When they got there, the security guards were gone. Donny whipped out his cell. "Hey, Ben, nobody's at the house."

He pressed the button. A response came right away. "Donny, we got a report of a break-in at the winery. We're there now."

"Damn it, Ben. That was a diversion. Secure things over there and send a couple of guys to the house."

"Okay, Donny. Right away!"

"Should we go inside?" Chris asked.

Donny twisted around in his seat. "No, we'll go to the clearing. I don't want to wait for my guys to get here."

Zora glanced behind her. She didn't see any move-ment, but the rumble of the truck behind them was growing louder. "Let's get out of here."

"But Mac didn't want Zora at the challenge. Maybe they want us to go to the clearing so they can ambush everyone," Chris said.

"I doubt it. But we'll have to take the chance. If they've got something bigger planned, they'll have to fight the whole pride." He shifted the gear again and they sped off, sending bits of gravel flying as they raced across the courtyard.

Mac only had to wait about ten minutes for his mother and father to arrive in their jeep. His father was dressed in dark pants and a white tunic with mul-ticolored embroidery around the deep U-neck. His mother wore a simple, sleeveless white dress. Mac trot-ted out to the middle of the clearing to wait for his father to start the challenge. He shook out his mane and sat facing the spectators.

Stephen strode into the center of the field and stopped a few steps away from Mac. "This is my last duty as leader of the MacKinnon pride. My mother, Lena and my father, Mackenzie passed it on to me. Now my son, named after his grandfather, will meet this challenge on my behalf."

The assemblage politely clapped as he returned to the sidelines. It amused Mac that it was a much quieter response than he'd heard from them when they'd witnessed his mating with Zora.

Murmurs ran through the crowd. A moment later, he saw movement as some of the spectators made an opening to let someone through. It was Eldon, trotting like he didn't have a care in the world.

In response, Mac bared his teeth and growled at him. But wait...where were the rest of Eldon's followers? Mac scanned the faces of the spectators clustered along the sidelines. No unfamiliar faces. None of Eldon's people were here to support him.

If they weren't here, they had to be somewhere else on the property. But where? Had they managed to track Zora? No, he had to push that from his mind. He couldn't lose this fight. Whatever Eldon was up to, Donny and Chris would be able to protect her.

Stephen lifted his arms towards the sky. "Let it begin!"

As they bounced along in the truck, Zora kept an eye on their pursuers. Though the lion had given up the chase, the truck was still following. She dropped the rake on the floor and gripped the seat cushion. The road was uneven, and with each bump she was almost thrown off her seat.

"Why did they come after Zora? Eldon's not going to win the challenge," Chris said.

"I don't know what's going on," Donny replied. "They might not be that smart, but they keep catching us unaware."

Just as he said that, another jeep came barreling out of the bushes. Donny swerved and they were on two wheels for a few seconds, then came crashing back down.

Zora held out her hands to brace herself. As she was shoved forward, she felt her right wrist flex and absorb most of the shock. Gasping, she cradled her arm and cried out in pain.

Donny glanced behind him, but turned his attention to the road as the other jeep circled back around, trying to get him to swerve again.

"Zora!" Chris reached for her, but he was thrown forward.

She braced herself with her left arm as Donny evaded their pursuer, and managed to get enough traction to speed up and maneuver between two tall trees.

"I can't stay on the road!" Donny shouted. "Hold on." He wove through the bushes and twisted tree trunks, trying to maintain his speed while avoiding the obstructions.

Her wrist hurt like hell and it was already swelling up. "How much further?" A sharp pain shot up her arm as she clutched it.

"It's just up ahead. Are they still behind us?" Donny asked. "I'm going to stop before we run into something."

"I don't see them!" Zora yelled. Donny's driving had been completely crazy, but he'd managed to squeeze his small jeep through spaces she would never have driven through. At least they'd managed to shake off their pursuers.

As the jeep slowed, Chris sighed and wiped the sweat from his face. "Damn it, Donny. You drove like a madman."

"You're telling me." Donny turned off the engine and sagged in his seat. "So much for our plan. Let's get out of here before someone else jumps out of the bushes."

"Hey, the clearing's up ahead." Chris pointed to a break in the trees several feet away.

Donny jumped out and helped Zora as she climbed out of the back seat. "Let me see that." He examined her wrist, which was now twice its normal size. "We should go get the medic. She's here for the challenge."

"She's a vet, Donny." Chris joined them and gently probed the swelling with his index finger. "How's she going to help?"

"I don't know. But it's better than nothing."

"It must've started. I hear cheering." Sounds of roars and human voices were echoing through the woods. "Donny, I want to see what's happening," Zora said.

"As long as you stay back and don't let Mac see you. I don't want to distract him."

"He'll pick up her scent," Chris interjected. "Then he'll know something must be wrong."

"We can't hide her! That didn't work, did it?"

Zora sighed as they glared at each other. This wasn't helping. "Stop fighting both of you! Can't we wait over there by the trees? That way I can see him and stay out of the way."

Both men stared at her again with the same expression of disbelief she'd seen from them back at the cottage. If they were shocked she was speaking up, they'd better get used to it.

"Wait here, Zora. I'll see what's going on," Chris said.

"No, I'll go and you wait here!" Donny ordered.

With her wrist throbbing she was in no mood for this nonsense. "Be quiet both of you!" she yelled, as she stamped her foot. "I'll wait here. Would one of you please go get the medic and bring her back?"

"I'll go!" Donny trotted towards the clearing.

"Sorry, Zora. Does it hurt bad?" Chris asked, as he reached over to touch her wrist again.

"Yes, so please don't touch it."

He froze, his fingers poised. "Oh, okay." Sheepish, he put his hands behind his back.

"You two!"

Zora spun around and gasped. It was Eldon's cousin Larry.

He strolled towards them, his stomach jiggling under his sweat-stained t-shirt. "Step aside, Chris. She's coming with me!"

Cheers rang in Mac's ears as he faced Eldon. Teeth bared, ears back, he crouched and prepared to spring.

Eldon barreled towards him, but before he reached Mac, he darted and ran off to the side. What was he doing? Mac sped after him, nipping at Eldon's tail. But yet again, Eldon swerved, leaving Mac having to stop himself in mid-run.

Skidding, he dug his claws into the grass to stop himself. Why wasn't he engaging? Instead, all he was doing was getting Mac to run in circles while he tried to catch up to him.

Wait a minute. That was obviously the plan. Eldon wanted to tire him out, get him to use up his energy so he wouldn't be able to defend himself.

Mac's heart hammered in his chest, as he gulped in air. Moving around as an adult lion took effort. As much as he'd tried to prepare himself, it was draining to keep up speed for long periods. He'd have to conserve his energy and find a way to end this quickly.

Eldon raced towards him again, and again he swerved at the last minute. Mac roared in frustration, circling Eldon. Calls and yells from the sidelines were drowned out as he blocked out everything going on around him. His only desire was to give Eldon a swipe or two. Or he could bite him hard enough to draw blood.

With a roar, Eldon shook his mane and charged again. This time Mac swerved and ran right into his opponent. Eldon stopped short and skidded as he tried to get away. Cheers and shouts filled the air.

Obviously, Eldon didn't want a direct confrontation. Whatever it was about, Mac was tired of it. He accelerated, turning the spectators into a blur of color as he raced around the clearing. Gaining speed, he cut off the area so Eldon couldn't try to dart away. Opening his jaws, Mac prepared to sink his teeth into his opponent's hindquarters. With any luck, Eldon wouldn't be able to sit down for months.

"Get moving, Larry!" Chris warned. "Leave us alone."

"Not yet. She's coming with me," he huffed. "The others ran off. Bunch of cowards. But I'm not going anyplace until Eldon pays me my money. And he's not paying unless she gets snatched."

Chris jumped in front of her. "Mac's just a few feet away. Want me to get him?"

"If Mac comes here that stops the challenge--and Eldon wins by default." Larry wiped sweat off his face with the back of his hand. "Just hand her over. Eldon's going to make Mac pay to get her back."

"Ransom? You're crazy if you think I'm going anywhere with you!" Zora yelled.

"You'll get paid too, Chris. When your brother takes over, he'll get everything and you'll get nothing. Aren't you tired of being passed over? Don't be stupid."

"If you leave now, I won't tell Mac to tear you apart," Chris sneered.

A roar sounded from the clearing, followed by cheers. She had to get out there.

"Eldon's keeping Mac busy." Larry advanced. "I don't care who wins, I just want the money I was promised. So hand her over right now!"

The next thing she knew, Chris launched himself and hit Larry so hard that they both fell to the ground.

Zora took her chance and bolted towards the clearing. As she ran out into the open, a lion charged towards her, his teeth bared. The other lion launched himself from the opposite direction, his powerful legs outstretched. Which one was Mac? Zora skidded and hit the ground, rolling out of the way as the lion landed just inches from where she'd been.

Someone screamed and everything around her went into slow motion. When she looked up, she saw a lion directly in front of her, his yellowish eyes narrowed. His long, pointed teeth glistening, he crouched and began to advance. Leaning on her swollen wrist, she tried to scamper to her feet, but she slid in the soft dirt.

The lion tossed his mane and let out a loud roar, his huge tongue licking back and forth. Frozen to the spot, she didn't have the breath to scream as the snarling beast rushed towards her. Eldon was about to have his revenge.

18 KILL OR BE KILLED

Focused on his opponent, Mac had been within inches of making contact with Eldon when he saw a blur rush out on the field. What the hell? No one was allowed out here without forfeiting the challenge. With a start he realized it was Zora!

Mac leaped over her. She rolled and tried to get her footing, but kept sliding. Eldon advanced on her, his teeth bared. Fury fueling him, Mac put himself between Zora and Eldon.

Growling, he lowered his body and bared his teeth. Preparing to spring and grab Eldon by the throat, he remained crouched, ears back and tail twitching, sending the message that he wasn't going to stop at drawing blood.

An explosion of noise surrounded him. Yelling and calls for him to finish Eldon, were mingled with warnings to Zora to get up and make for the sidelines.

Animal instinct took over, prodding him to rip Eldon apart for daring to threaten his mate. If he'd been a lion in the wild, Mac would've extracted a worse punishment and left him emasculated, literally.

Obviously realizing he was in trouble, Eldon backed up as Mac advanced. Adrenaline surged through him, fueling Mac's desire to put an end to this once and for all. Vanquish this threat to his mate and his pride. *Kill him now. Kill him. Kill him.*

He sprung and flew through the air, landing on top of Eldon, pinning him down so he couldn't sprint away. Mac dragged his claws along Eldon's side, scoring him practically down to his tailbone. Eldon screeched in terror and he fought to free himself from Mac's grasp.

Kill him now. Finish him. Do it now.

"Mac, please!" Zora screamed. "Stop it!"

Zora's voice infiltrated the red hot urge to destroy his enemy. He raised his head and searched for her, but his vision was hazy. It was time to finish this. Eldon must never be a threat again.

The crowd fell silent, and the only sound left was the steady vibration of his heart and Eldon's deep breaths.

Kill him now. Do it now. Now.

Suddenly Zora's face swam into view as she approached, clutching one arm to her chest. Her t-shirt and shorts were mud-covered and blood dripped from her knee. He sniffed her scent and smelled her fear. Was it fear of him? Or of what he was about to do?"

She stopped just steps away. "Mac, let him go. You've won."

No. He couldn't stop. He had to finish it. His animal nature cried out, hungry for triumph and for blood. Kill or be killed.

"Please," she whispered.

Seeing the tears in her eyes stirred the human man within him. Zora was safe. He could stop now. She was safe.

"Son. It's over," Stephen called out. "Let him go."

Mac backed off. As soon as he was free, Eldon scampered away to the sidelines. Out of the corner of his eye, Mac saw a woman in blue scrubs crouching next to him.

"Mac?"

Zora's gentle voice steadied him. But he didn't dare get too close to her. Not yet. The scent of blood was still too fresh, and he couldn't be sure what he might do. Step by step, he inched closer and closer. Even as he fought it, he was drawn to her.

Inhaling her sweet scent, he felt calm returning, ordering his thoughts. Dropping down in front of her, he fell onto his side. While he struggled to release the blood lust that still consumed him, he felt his body transforming. Bone and sinew strained and contorted into the form of his human body. When it was over, he rolled into a fetal position, shivering as the cool air hit his skin.

Zora dropped down to her knees and gathered him up, propping him against her. "Come back, baby. Please."

Human. If it meant being with her, he'd be human again. "Zora," he croaked, surprised at the gravely sound of his own voice. "Are you all right?"

"I'm fine. Just rest." She caressed his cheek. "It's all right now."

Exhausted, Mac leaned his head against her chest and closed his eyes. Yes, everything would be all right now that they were together.

An hour later Zora was at Mac's bedside, watching as Dr. Linda Garcia finished her examination. She pulled the sheet over his chest and grabbed her duffle bag. Donny and Chris had brought him to the house in Donny's jeep. Mac had been incoherent while they'd cleaned the blood off him and put him to bed.

"Heart rate is returning to normal. He's recovering quickly. Just let him rest," she said, tucking a strand of light brown hair behind her ear. "It would be a good idea if he visits his vet when he gets back home."

"His vet is my sister." Zora eased off the bed. "I'll make sure he goes."

"Oh, good idea to keep it in the family. There's a small network of doctors who treat shifters. I'm glad that he's got one nearby." She slung the strap across her shoulder. Even though she was petite, she had no problem with the bulky bag. "Don't put any strain on that wrist. It's just a sprain, but it has to heal."

"Thank you, Dr. Garcia. You treat humans too?"

"Call me, Linda," she said. "I was a paramedic before I became a vet. One of my friends from school is a shifter. That's how I found out about them. He recruited me to be part of the doctors' network. What's your sister's name? I might know her."

"Diane Hill. She has a practice with her husband, Michael," Zora replied, wincing as a pain shot up her arm. It figured that just mentioning her sister's name would make her wrist hurt.

"Oh yes. I've heard of a Dr. Hill in Bristol Hills. That's your sister?" Small crinkles formed in the corners of her eyes as she smiled. "We have to be careful about sharing information and keeping records. If it were to get out, it would expose everyone to danger."

"Yes, I know," Zora admitted. She'd heard enough about that from her sister.

"By the way, I heard the good news." Linda patted Zora's shoulder. "Congratulations on your mating."

How had she heard about it so quickly? "Were you at the waterfall?" Zora asked.

"No, I just got here this morning to be on hand in case they needed me. I saw the news posted on one of the lion shifter message boards. The community is pretty tight-knit. They keep each other updated." Linda grinned, as she opened the door.

Zora had made the choice to mate with Mac in front of everyone and she wasn't ashamed of it. But knowing that gossip about it was spreading beyond the MacKinnon pride would take some getting used to.

Before Linda could leave the room, Cynthia walked up. "How's Mac? Will he be okay?" she asked.

"He'll be fine, Cynthia. I've got to get going," Linda replied. "I'll see myself out."

"Bye, Linda. And thanks," Zora said, relieved that Mac would be okay.

"They want you downstairs. There's a family meeting," Cynthia said, as she looked over at Mac. "You'll be back before he wakes up."

"I don't want to leave him."

"You have to come down, Zora. You're Mac's mate."

Yes, she was his mate now. Since he couldn't be at the meeting, she had a responsibility. "Okay, let's go."

Cynthia led her to the study, a large rectangular, window-lined room off the main entrance hall. An imposing carved wooden desk sat at one end, and two cherry wood bookcases sat behind it. On the shelves were sets of crystal glasses and wine labels displayed in silver frames.

At the opposite end of the study, two couches and two overstuffed chairs were arranged around a flat coffee table. Mac's father and Chris sat on one couch, Ellen on another. She patted the space next to her as Zora approached.

"How are you dear?" Ellen asked, a tight smile on her lips.

"I'm fine," she lied. It was hard to be calm with Mac lying upstairs.

"Zora, I'm glad you could join us," Stephen said. "I want you to hear what they have to say." He motioned to Cynthia, who was standing by the door. "Send them in."

Seconds later, two security officers entered with Eldon's cousin Larry between them. The officers, both muscular like Donny, wore badges on their uniforms and had the same no-nonsense expression. Larry, visibly shaken, tried to pull away, but was held fast.

"Where's Eldon?" Mac's father asked.

"Donny's bringing him," Cynthia replied. "And Eldon's father just arrived. He wants to join you."

"Matthew's here? He got my message then. Send him in."

Cynthia went out into the entry hall again, and when she returned, an older man wearing a dark blue suit was with her. His mane of pure white hair hung to his shoulders. Although he didn't look much older than

Mac's father, his face was gaunt and hollowed, like he'd been drained of energy. He sat in one of the over-stuffed chairs.

"Matthew. I'm sorry you have to be here for this," Stephen said.

Instead of replying, Matthew nodded, his eyes downcast.

"What do you want from me? I was doing what El-don told me to do," Larry blurted out. "I didn't want to kidnap her. It wasn't my idea."

"Admit it. He offered you money to kidnap Zora," Ellen snapped. "Then you attacked Chris."

"No! I was trying to get away! I swear it. Right Chris? No hard feelings."

Chris gave him a look of disbelief, his fists clenched. "No hard feelings? You're an asshole!"

Larry squirmed. "Eldon didn't want to fight Mac. He was going to run around a lot then give up like he surrendered. While he was at the challenge, we were supposed to snatch her." He pointed to Zora. "Then Mac would have to pay to get her back. It's all Eldon's fault. But I swear I didn't want to do it!" Larry struggled to get away from the guards, but they held him without putting up any effort.

Donny entered the room dragging Eldon by the collar. His face was scratched but the rest of the marks from Mac's claws were hidden under his white button-down shirt.

"Get off me!" Eldon stopped in his tracks when he saw his father. "Dad! What are you doing here? I told you I could handle things."

"You handled them, didn't you?" Matthew spat. "I was wrong to let this challenge go on. You did it all for money."

"No, dad. They're lying. You believe them over me?" Eldon squeaked, sounding like a spoiled child.

"Larry told us your plan. Your buddies ran off and left you two here," Mac's father countered. "You've violated the challenge laws, Eldon."

Eldon threw his shoulders back and glared at Stephen. "What are you going to do about it? You think you're important because you have money!"

"I gave you everything," Matthew said.

"You stupid old man. Where's my inheritance? You wasted it on those bad deals. That was my money!" Eldon tried to get away from Donny, but only managed to free one arm. "Yes, I challenged the high and mighty MacKinnons. And I would've won if Mac hadn't cheated!"

"Cheated? He kicked your ass!" Chris retorted.

"He cheated. He sent his mate out there to distract me. You did this!" He pointed at Zora.

Her heart racing, Zora jumped out of her seat. "Larry told us everything about your plan to kidnap me!" How could he blame her for this shit? After what she and Mac had been through, she was pissed.

"Zora, dear." Ellen touched her arm. "Don't let him upset you any further. He's not worth it."

"Not worth it? I'm as good as Mac is!" Eldon yelled. "Mac taunted me when he mated with you at that waterfall. You and Mac made me look like a fool in front of my friends!"

Zora shivered, suddenly feeling very vulnerable. Even with Donny holding Eldon, he looked menacing. His face and neck were flushed dark red as he shook with anger.

"You will not insult this family!" Stephen came to his feet, his shoulders back.

"Be quiet, Eldon!" Matthew ordered. "You've said enough."

"All my life you compared me to Mac. Why can't you be more like him? Why can't you go to college and get an MBA? Why don't you do this? Why don't you do that? I hate him and I hate you!"

Matthew jumped out of his chair and smacked Eldon across the face. "You've embarrassed me and the Durant pride. We're going home."

Realizing that maybe he might have gone too far, he dodged out of his father's way as the older man reached out to grab him. But Donny pushed him into Matthew's arms.

"Come home now!" Matthew yanked him like he was a toddler, dragging him out of the study.

Donny and the other security officers followed, with Larry in tow. Eldon's curses could be heard until the front door closed behind them.

Zora sighed. For all his posturing, Eldon was little more than a child in a man's body. "What's going to happen to him?" she asked.

"Matthew will punish him, I suspect," Stephen replied. "He won't be the pride leader, though. They've lost so many members that it'll probably disband."

Ellen sucked her teeth. "Matthew should have put his foot down with Eldon in the beginning."

"Yes, I know," Stephen agreed. "But it's too late to fix it now."

As long as she never had to see Eldon or his obnoxious cousin again, Zora would be happy. All she wanted was for Mac to recover and then they could start their lives together as mates.

19 PARTNERS

After the meeting, Zora joined the family on the back patio for lunch. Some of the pride members were there too, and they greeted her and offered their congratulations. Unfortunately, she wasn't very hungry, and after forcing down half a sandwich, she headed back upstairs.

She thought Mac was asleep when she entered the bedroom, but as soon as she closed the door, his eyes snapped open.

"Where were you?" he asked, stretching his arms over his head. "Why are you wearing a sling?"

"I sprained my wrist," she replied, as she came to the side of the bed. "I'll fill you in later." There was no need to go into it right now. She didn't want him getting upset again.

"Where's Eldon?"

"I'll fill you in on that later too. Now rest."

"I'm cold. Got used to the fur, I guess." He pulled the sheet up to his neck. "Babe, why did you run out on the field like that? You could've been killed."

"I'll tell you after you rest."

Groaning, he stretched again. This time he stuck his leg out from under the covers. "Okay, I'll rest if you rest with me."

Oh yes, Mac was coming back. When she reached for the blanket, he waved her away.

"Take off your clothes first," he said.

"Mac, you're not in any shape for--"

"Off." Smiling, he folded his arms across his chest. "Now."

"Excuse me, what is this? Alpha lion shit?"

"Yup. When the king asks his queen to get naked, he expects compliance." He grinned, obviously enjoying himself. "So take off those clothes, get into bed and let's snuggle."

Not a bad idea. In fact, she loved it. After everything they'd been through, she was desperate to feel his arms around her. "If you want me naked, you've got to help me." She pointed to the sling.

"I'm always undressing you, aren't I?" Mac threw back the covers and sprung from the bed, but staggered as he came to his feet."

"Are you all right? What is it?" Zora asked.

"Just got up too fast, that's all," he replied, as he steadied himself. "Don't worry, I can handle this."

He gave her a peck on the forehead while he removed her sling. "Hey, your wrist is swollen."

"That's why I had a sling on." She braced her hand on his chest. "I told you, I'll explain it all later. Now help me get this shirt off."

"Right away." He gently pulled it over her head, and then tossed it on the floor.

"Why are you always throwing my clothes around?"

"Because I want you naked and I don't have time to waste," he teased. "Come over here." He sat on the bed and reached behind her to unhook her bra. "Why are these always so hard to open?"

"Don't you dare break my--" Before she got the words out, he'd pulled it open, got it off her and sent the bra flying across the room.

Mac!" Why couldn't he just unhook the thing?

"Don't be mad, babe. When lion shifters see what they want, they go after it." He licked his lips, then took her breast into his mouth and sucked hard.

Her breath caught in her throat as she melted against him. As much as she wanted more, they both needed to rest. "We're supposed to be snuggling," she murmured.

"I know. But I'm hungry." Meeting her gaze, he licked her nipple. "Besides, I'm not finished. I only did one."

"No!" Laughing, she wrapped her arms across her chest, careful not to hurt her wrist. "Just help me get my shorts off. Then no more licking!"

"What about sucking? Or kissing?" he teased, his hazel eyes shining.

"Kissing, maybe. But nothing else until you're rested." Which she hoped would be very soon.

"If you insist," he smirked. He undid her shorts without having to break anything. Easing his fingers under her panties, he smoothed both garments down over her hips. She stepped out of them, his hands supporting her.

"Another spanking?" he asked, as he squeezed her butt. "We need to do that more often."

"We? I'm the one who got spanked," she retorted.

"And you enjoyed it." He got back into bed and eased her down next to him. Careful to arrange her so her injured wrist was above the covers, he pulled her into his arms and threw his leg across her for good measure.

"How's your back?" he asked.

"Itching. I might need more of that aloe," she replied.

"I wouldn't mind going back to the waterfall for some other things."

"I'll bet," she replied. Neither would she. But for now, she was enjoying being in his arms.

"Mind if we leave for home later? I don't want to wait until tomorrow," he said.

"As long as you feel better, I'm fine with it."

"Good. I have to check on things at the new shop." He rubbed his leg against hers. "Hope they were able to make progress."

"What about the pride, Mac? How are you going to lead it when you're back in Bristol Hills?"

"I'm going to ask Donny to watch over things here. Chris isn't ready yet." Mac sighed. "It'll be better this way. Then my folks can concentrate on running the winery."

"The doctor said you should make an appointment with Diane when you get back. But I think I should tell you, last time we met we had a fight." Zora felt her stomach drop at the thought of facing her sister again. "She's not going to be happy we mated."

"Give her time, Zora. She has to accept it," he said. "And your folks too."

"I know." How would she tell them? At least she wouldn't have to explain to them what shifters were. But that didn't mean they'd like what she'd done. She only hoped that her conversation with them didn't turn out like her confrontation with Diane.

"Don't worry, babe. Just let things play out," he said.

Mac was right. There was no need to worry about it now. It would work out, though it might take a while.

Leaning her head on his chest, she sniffed. "You need a shower."

He chuckled. "Don't like gamey smelling men? What kind of mate are you?"

"A mate who loves you," she replied.

"Then I'm one lucky man, because I love you too."

Nestled in his arms, she listened to his heartbeat. It was strong and reassuring, just like he was. Mac was her mate and nothing would ever come between them. They were partners in life and in love.

Family Pride: Blood Fever

Coming in August 2015
Part 2 in the Family Pride series

After claiming Zora Mason as his mate, and fighting
off a threat to the MacKinnon pride, Mac is more than
ready to get back to managing his coffee bar and settling into mated bliss. But just when it looks like
things are quieting down, Mac and Zora find more
challenges ahead.

Plans for Zora and Mac's official introduction the to
the pride, and the opening of the new coffee bar may
be derailed when, gripped by a mysterious blood fever
lingering after the leadership challenge, Mac is driven
to the edge of his endurance as he fights to keep his
inner lion under control.

Juggling her responsibilities in the business and her
position as the mate of the pride leader becomes even
more challenging when Zora is forced to confront her
fear that Mac is changing into someone she doesn't
recognize.

As the fever pushes Mac to the edge, the revelation of an old, painful family secret proves to be the key to saving Mac's life. Zora and Mac come up with a plan to end the threat of the fever forever, but that same plan can destroy them both.

Is their love strong enough to defeat the blood fever, so they can live happily ever after as mates?

OTHER BOOKS BY DEBORAH A BAILEY

Science Fiction Romance Available in E-book, Print &
Audio

Hathor Legacy: Outcast
Hathor Legacy: Burn
Electric Dreams: Seven Futuristic Tales

ABOUT THE AUTHOR

Deborah A Bailey's Science Fiction Romance and Paranormal Romance novels include suspense, a bit of mystery and a lot of romantic heat.

Her other published works include Hathor Legacy: Outcast, Hathor Legacy: Burn (books one and two in the Hathor Legacy universe) a short story collection, Electric Dreams: Seven Futuristic Tales, three nonfiction books, and articles for various online publications.

Visit her site http://www.BrightStreetBooks.com/ and subscribe for the newsletter (and download a free short story) so you'll be the first to hear about giveaways, book launches and lots of information for readers and writers!